Was Charlot him?

Isaiah couldn't he
expression change... She'd been angry when
he'd approached the paddock, but not now. She
was caring. Lovely. Beautiful.

When he reached a hand to her cheek, she
almost leaned into it. But not quite.

Instead she took a firm step back. "Don't mess
with my head, cowboy."

He lifted one eyebrow.

"And don't do your strong, silent cowboy
nonsense on me, either. I'm here to do a job, and
I've already managed to tuck myself into a very
Hatfield-and-McCoy-style land feud and into
your family scandal, and I've created a chasm
between me and the old-guard veterinarian. I
don't need casual flirting to muddy the already
churning waters."

"No one mentioned the word *casual*."

She shot him a skeptical look as she came
around the front of the horse.

"And for the record?" He paused just ahead
of her, blocking her way. "I don't do anything
casual. Ever."

Multipublished bestselling author **Ruth Logan Herne** loves God, her country, her family, dogs, chocolate and coffee! Married to a very patient man, she lives in an old farmhouse in Upstate New York and thinks possums should leave the cat food alone and snakes should always live outside. There are no exceptions to either rule! Visit Ruth at ruthloganherne.com.

Books by Ruth Logan Herne

Love Inspired

Shepherd's Crossing

Her Cowboy Reunion
A Cowboy in Shepherd's Crossing
Healing the Cowboy's Heart

Grace Haven

An Unexpected Groom
Her Unexpected Family
Their Surprise Daddy
The Lawman's Yuletide Baby
Her Secret Daughter

Kirkwood Lake

The Lawman's Second Chance
Falling for the Lawman
The Lawman's Holiday Wish
Loving the Lawman
Her Holiday Family

Visit the Author Profile page at Harlequin.com for more titles.

Healing the Cowboy's Heart

Ruth Logan Herne

H HARLEQUIN® LOVE INSPIRED®

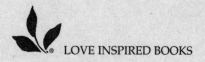

LOVE INSPIRED BOOKS

Recycling programs for this product may not exist in your area.

ISBN-13: 978-1-335-53929-8

Healing the Cowboy's Heart

www.Harlequin.com

Printed in U.S.A.

He that covereth his sins shall not prosper:
but who so confesseth and forsaketh them
shall have mercy.
—*Proverbs* 28:13

This book is dedicated to my good friend Becky Prophet. We share three grandchildren and a love of God and good stories. Becky, the good Lord sure blessed us when He brought you into the family. This one's for you. Thank you for being a great "Mimi" and a great friend.

Chapter One

Charlotte Fitzgerald might be a big-animal vet, schooled to remain unemotional when things go bad, but the scene in front of her sent a chill of misgiving through her despite the Idaho mid-summer's day. She was facing seven critically ill horses who had found their way into a paddock adjacent to a well-known riding academy at the height of summer-camp season. On her right were a dozen young steeplechasers, hoping and praying for the stray horses' survival.

Charlotte had spent a lot of years praying as a child. Wishing her mom hadn't died shortly after giving birth to her. Hoping her father would become the kind of dad every child wanted and needed.

But her Mama did die and her prayers regarding her father went unanswered. As a result the intuitive horsewoman and veterinary surgeon learned to stand on her own two feet. For now that was enough.

"That one needs to go down." Braden Hirsch had been the only local farm-animal vet until Charlotte rolled her mobile-veterinary-clinic van into town less than forty-eight hours before to fulfill the terms of her uncle's will: if she spends a year helping to keep Pine Ridge Ranch solvent, she would inherit 25 percent of the ranch's value next summer. She'd give the mixed horse and sheep venture free veterinary care as needed, but right now her focus was here, watching the crusty vet perform a half-hearted medical triage on the depleted animals.

She'd intended to meet Dr. Hirsch later today, a polite gesture. One professional to the other. He was in his sixties, according to the internet, and maybe considering retirement.

Only here they were, caught at a scene of horrific neglect and tragic circumstances, and she was about to make the whole thing worse by disagreeing with him.

He jerked a thumb toward a hobbling chestnut gelding. "Too far gone." Then he waved to a group of three miserable creatures that were huddled together. "The palomino might have a chance. The rest..." He scowled at the remaining horses, and Charlotte understood his expression.

He wasn't mad at them.

He was furious that they'd been left to struggle for however long it took to put them in this wretched condition.

"Braden." The woman who'd called for help kept her voice purposely soft. "You're going to put six of them down?"

He glared at her, then the horses. "You wanted a professional opinion, Bitsy. You got it. Any idea where they came from?"

She shook her head. "None. Which means they've probably been wandering throughout winter, based on the state they're in. You'd think that with the conditions we've had for the last two months, they'd have recovered somewhat, wouldn't you?"

The veterinarian huffed. "Some are smart enough to do that. Some aren't. And sometimes it becomes survival of the fittest."

Survival of the fittest? Char bit back a protest. He was wrong.

Char was sure of it, but she was the new kid on the block, just arrived from veterinary school and a stint on a Western New York farm specializing in horse care. There was no way these seven had been open grazing anywhere for the past few months, because they'd have had abundant food and water, even if rain had been scarce. And they would have been noticed, wouldn't they?

"What do you think, Doctor?" The woman turned toward Charlotte, seeking a second opinion. An opinion that wasn't going to win her any points with the other veterinarian. She began to answer as a pair of sheriff's cars pulled into the equine academy's driveway, followed by a pickup truck hauling a two-horse trailer.

The older vet's narrowed eyes challenged her to disagree. The last thing she wanted was to begin her new career on the wrong side of the established veterinary practice, but she put her comfort on hold to do what was best for the horses. "Where there's life, there's hope."

The woman—Bitsy Armbruster—let out a sigh of relief as Chad Armbruster tried to distract the campers behind them. There were about a dozen teens and preteens in attendance, and whatever happened next wasn't something a bunch of horse-loving kids needed to see.

A man climbed out of the pickup truck and came their way. He walked big. Straight. Tall. Sure of himself and square-shouldered. Crazy good-looking. Black hair, a touch long, as if taking time to get haircuts didn't make the short list. Great cheekbones and a square jaw suggested Native American lineage. Warrior shoulders completed the image.

"Isaiah!" One of the girl campers jumped the fence and tore across the pasture. "I knew you'd come!" She threw her arms around him and held on tight, and when he hugged her back, the look of love he gave her…

Charlotte would have given anything for a father who loved her like that. She got a cheating conniver instead, a man who came from money and managed to lose it all once he was running the family publishing business. She had learned a lot as the youngest daughter of an esteemed Kentucky horse-breeding family, though. She went into veterinary school at Cornell with an intimate knowledge of horses. That knowledge was about to put her toe to toe with the old man at her side.

"Isaiah." Bitsy motioned him their way. "I'm so glad you've come. And you brought a trailer." Hope raised her voice slightly.

The girl started to come forward with him.

The man paused, saw Dr. Hirsch's expression, then indicated the other side of the fence with a simple thrust of his chin. His message was clear. Would the girl follow the silent directive?

She frowned, then trudged across the field and hopped the fence to join the other campers on their way to a barn set a fair distance away.

Neat trick, thought Charlotte.

"I don't think you'll be needing that trailer, Isaiah," said the old man.

"Better prepared than wishing I was, Braden." He kept his voice low, and walked with quiet authority. "If I left it at home, J.J. would think I made up my mind before I took the time to have a look, and what kind of man does that?" He didn't look like he expected an answer and didn't get one. He indicated the electric fencing surrounding the pasture. "Has anyone blocked the way they got in here?"

"We called the sheriff as soon as we discovered them," Bitsy answered, "but both deputies were at the other end of the county and we didn't want to leave either the campers or the horses unsupervised, so I asked Ty Carrington to help," she explained. "He knew that Charlotte had just come to town to open a veterinary practice, so he asked her to come over. He's fixing the fencing on the northwest corner. He'll give us a high sign when we're ready to power up. We had shut the power down to save money because our horses are kept closer to the practice jump areas right now."

"So, breaking through the wire wasn't a big challenge."

"No."

Bitsy's phone buzzed a text. She read it and gave them a thumbs-up. "Fencing is powered up."

"A lot of waiting for horses who aren't likely to try to get anywhere fast," said Braden. "I've got office hours in thirty. Let's get this done." He began moving forward with a worn black bag.

"Hold on." Charlotte crossed the distance quickly and stood between him and the first horse. "You're going to put them down without giving them any kind of examination?"

Braden huffed, impatient. "I might not have a fancy van with pretty letters on the side, but I've got eyes and experience, girl. That's what bears weight around here."

The other man—Isaiah—took a moment to look behind them. She'd parked her brand-new mobile veterinary van on the back side of the Armbruster house. The words *CMF VETERI-NARY* stood out in a large font, over the peaceable image of a horse, a cow and an ewe with lambs. A trusty dog sat off to the side, while a mother cat looked after tumbling kittens. He studied the van, then her without a speck of emotion for either.

Charlotte stood her ground. "They deserve the courtesy of an examination."

The older man glared at her, then Bitsy. "I came here as a favor."

Bitsy swallowed hard but sided with Charlotte. "We should check them over, shouldn't we, Braden? If you don't have time, maybe Charlotte would do it for us."

Charlotte motioned toward the sad-looking group of horses. Six were standing, listless, as if too tired to walk or eat. The seventh was down, on her side, an aged mare that might have been pretty in her day. She wasn't pretty now. "I'd be happy to do the exams, Doctor, so you can get to your office hours on time."

He glared at her, then the horses, then her again. He turned as if to leave, then swung back. "Let's get to it." Sour-faced, he started for a horse.

"We've made him angry." Bitsy sounded genuinely distraught, as if the old veterinarian's anger was a bigger worry than it should be. "I didn't mean to do that."

Neither had Charlotte, but to declare such a permanent decision without making an examination seemed wrong.

"Braden has given years of time and expertise to help reestablish the ranches in this part of Idaho," Bitsy added as they followed the old man. "I'd never want to hurt his feelings."

"Put the blame on me," declared Charlotte, and she didn't keep her voice all that soft, either. "Because if I'm going to have half a dozen dead horses on my conscience, it's going to be for a good reason."

Bitsy looked surprised, but then not so surprised, as Charlotte's words hit home.

The cowboy tipped back his hat slightly. He met her gaze briefly, then moved up alongside the older vet. "How can I help, Braden?"

A peacemaker.

Well, good for him. Charlotte had a lot of respect for a serene existence, but the cheating father and then the law-breaking ex-boyfriend made her realize that peace at any cost wasn't peace. It was capitulation, and where these poor horses were concerned, she wasn't about to give an inch.

The cowboy turned. "Do we have any placements, Bitsy?"

"The Council Rescue can take two."

The old vet snorted.

Bitsy ignored the sound as Charlotte moved forward to examine the horse.

"Ty said they could house two for the interim."

The old vet shot her an incredulous look over his shoulder.

"Young Eagle texted that he could take one and his sister would tend another. He's coming right down."

Braden Hirsch's scowl deepened. "A couple of weeks back, that might have been the way to go, but I'm telling you straight, you're causing more harm than good to try to rehabilitate animals like this. You get 'em healthy and then someone tries to ride one and gets thrown because the horse has lost its trust of humans or just spooks easy, and then your happy ending goes up in smoke."

"It's a valid point." Char felt the heat in the first horse's leg, then moved on to the group of three. They scattered, but they scattered quickly enough to make her assessment fairly easy. "Any horse that can shy that quickly deserves a chance."

"Being scared doesn't make them healthy, girl."

"Doctor," she replied smoothly. "And I have the Cornell University diploma to prove it."

"High-faluting schools don't always mean good," he retorted. "Sometimes they just mean overpriced and overdressed."

Two men had joined Bitsy. They were putting halters on the horses to aid in moving them, but when they approached a dun gelding, Charlotte shook her head. The dun was too far gone for help at this point. And that left them with the inert horse on the ground.

"Oh, baby, I'm so sorry." Char ran a gentle hand along the horse's neck when she got to the prone Appaloosa. "So very sorry." She did a quick exam. The mare's heart and lungs sounded fair, but she was little more than bones. Bones and...in foal, Charlotte realized.

And yet so debilitated at this point that the idea of getting her healthy enough to have the foal, much less care for it, seemed impossible.

A shadow fell over her. She looked up.

Isaiah shifted slightly, then squatted beside her. He didn't try to hide his brokenhearted expression. He laid a hand along the horse's neck as if in benediction, then met Char's gaze. "Two to put down? And five to attempt healing."

She started to nod when the horse lifted her head. Looked around. She seemed disoriented for brief seconds, then rolled slightly to see Isaiah.

He stared at the mare.

The mare gazed back.

And when the big Native American swallowed hard, Char had to fight off a thrust of rising emotion. "You know her."

Gaze firm, he laid a hand against the horse's face.

"She knows you." Char read the horse's reaction. And the man's.

He blinked once, a silent assent.

Braden came up behind them. "I knew this one was an easy decision, even for someone fresh out of the classroom." He stopped. Stared. Then his look went from the horse to Isaiah and back again. He swallowed hard. Really hard. "She can't be here. She was put down a long, long time ago."

Isaiah kept his face flat and a comforting hand along the horse's jaw. "Clearly not. But maybe that would have been the better choice, considering."

"I'll get things ready." Braden set down a medical bag that had seen better days and opened it. With shaking hands, he withdrew what he needed to inject the mare.

"No."

Braden paused. He stared at Isaiah. So did Charlotte.

"We're not putting her down. If she can get up and walk, we're not putting her down."

"Well, she can't or won't—stubborn to the end—and you know every reason why we can't let her live, Isaiah. Better than most."

Charlotte stayed quiet, but when Isaiah stood, tall and firm, she stood, too.

"Come along, Ginger. Come along."

The horse seemed to brighten up. She blew out a breath, stared up at him, then tried to roll.

She couldn't make it.

Her eyes went wide, as if the mare realized how much was riding on this single maneuver.

"Come along, girl. Home's waiting."

Braden rolled his eyes. "Standing or laying

isn't the question here. It's who she is, Isaiah. Some things are better left as is. You've got two kids on that ranch to think of. Neither one of your brother's kids deserves to be around a crazy horse that's hurt kids before."

"Hey, girl." The rugged cowboy ignored the old man's caution and stooped a little. "It's up to you. Stay? Or go?"

The horse stared up at him, as if weighing his words. Then with a mighty surge, she rolled fully and almost sprang to her feet, suddenly energized.

"Don't do this, Isaiah." Braden stood between the cowboy and the upright horse. "There's no reason to bring this all back up. It won't bring Alfie back, but it will rile up a whole lot of emotions for people we both love. Your mother. Your family. You know it as well as I do."

Isaiah smoothed a hand along the horse's scabby, dirt-crusted neck. "She'll come with me."

The old vet's eyes flashed. "I won't be a part of this, Isaiah. Not one part. You know what happened that day. We both do. You would bring this mistake back to your mother's door? Lay blame at her feet?"

The cowboy kept a light hand on the mare. "That's exactly why I have no choice."

"Isaiah." Braden changed his tone slightly. He

moved forward, imploring. "I'm your godfather, and I'm asking you. Begging you. Don't do this. Please. It's foolishness. It changes nothing, so what's the point? She's beyond help. Beyond hope. It's time to do the right thing."

The square-shouldered Native American faced the smaller doctor. His expression mixed remorse and conviction. "Which is why she's coming home with me. Live or die, she'll be where she should have been all along."

The old man grabbed his bag so hard that it banged Charlotte's leg, almost toppling her into the horse. "Out of my way!" He stormed past her and crossed the field, his bag half-open.

"I'm out." He barked the words at Bitsy, but made sure they all could hear as another horse trailer arrived. A local-news car followed. "And I hope your new horse vet does well by the lot of you because I won't be part of any of this nonsense."

Nonsense?

A flash of fear gripped Charlotte.

What if she lost them all? What kind of reputation as a horse-savvy vet would she have then? Was she laying her career on the line for a hopeless cause?

One of the men motioned for her.

She began to move that way.

The mare swayed, as if weak. Then she caught herself, drew up her neck and stood firm.

Charlotte did the same. She was in a way better spot than the horse, and if the horse could muster up courage, then so would the doctor.

Saving Ginger was nonsense?

Cool anger chilled Isaiah's veins, while the July temperature mounted.

The horse tipped her head and looked at him. If he'd had a choice, he lost it at that moment.

Bitsy approached with another halter. He ran his hand up the horse's nose and murmured soft words to her. Would the aged mare trust his words after being betrayed long ago? Did she really recognize him?

She leaned her poor, thin face into his hand and breathed softly, an equine sigh.

Maybe she knew him. Perhaps she'd forgiven him for standing by and saying nothing all those years ago. For letting her be taken because he was caught in a tough spot between the horse and his mother.

His mother.

She would recognize the horse. Maybe not initially, but once she filled out—if she lived—Stella Woods would recognize the horse she'd accused years ago. And that wouldn't go well.

Bitsy sweet-talked Ginger while the new veterinarian gathered information from Ty Carrington, Young Eagle and a woman from the horse rescue just south of Council. She offered initial instructions to each one as they guided the horses into their respective trailers. Curious, the campers had moseyed their way again once the horses were being loaded. The young doctor noticed that and glanced over her shoulder.

She was blonde. Blue-eyed. A lovely face, with the kind of figure that made a smart man take note, and wasn't that funny because he hadn't had time to take notice of a woman for a while. Partly his fault. Partly God's timing in parking two orphaned kids in his care.

So yes, she was beautiful with her long golden ponytail, a wisp of fringe around her cheeks and forehead, and the plain T-shirt over thin blue jeans. She'd chosen a good outfit for animal work and long summer days. But Idaho farms and ranches were tough by nature. To start off at odds with his godfather, a man who shared history with 90 percent of the area's ranchers, wasn't just risky. It probably sounded the death knell of her professional career, because the Hirsch family carried clout in Adams County and they weren't afraid to use it.

A second news car pulled in behind the sheriff's cruisers. Neglected farm animals were big news in Western Idaho and a case like this would make headlines. And if the rescues failed, his godfather would use those headlines to his own advantage.

Braden didn't like to be second-guessed. To have this young woman challenge his decisions wasn't something he would forgive easily, even though he sat in the front church pew every Sunday, with his wife and her sister right there beside him.

Ty and Young Eagle had situated their rigs to receive their cargo. Word had spread, more people arrived and Isaiah hung back purposely. As the other horses were being carefully loaded, the young veterinarian came his way. She stripped off her gloves and shoved them into a pocket before donning a new pair.

"Bitsy said your name is Charlotte?"

She nodded toward her van with a jut of her chin. "New big-animal vet in town and already making enemies with the establishment."

"Not all of the establishment." He noted the men loading trailers, Bitsy and the kids, none of whom had really stopped watching.

"And you are?"

"Isaiah Woods. Rancher. Horse breeder."

She frowned quickly. "Can you segregate her at your place so she's quarantined for the first few weeks, Mr. Woods? You don't want to track something into your herd."

"Isaiah. And yes. I've got a spot."

She accepted the correction with a brief nod. "You know this horse?"

"Yes."

She slanted a quick look of assessment his way. "And?"

He stayed silent.

She didn't. "You're Native American."

"Nimiipuu. Or Nez Percé, as we're known now."

"The Last Indian War."

Few people remembered the native history, how a band of Nez Percé was hunted over a thousand miles of rough terrain, caught after much fighting and then sequestered on a hot, dry plain in Oklahoma, far from their cooler mountainous homeland. She surprised him and he didn't surprise easily. "Someone paid attention in eighth-grade history. Many don't."

"Well, right now I'm paying attention to her." Charlotte moved along the mare's flank. She closed her eyes and gently probed the animal's body. "She's due to foal soon."

Now she got his attention. He stared at the horse, then followed the skinny line of her curvature until the familiar sway beneath her confirmed the doctor's diagnosis. "That can't be good for her."

"Babies do tend to steal whatever they need

from their mothers, leaving the mother drained. In her case, drained equates starving."

The horse gulped as if swallowing was hard.

"Do you have a place ready for her?" she asked as she smoothed her hand along the mare's flank.

"A hay barn with three stalls I use when I need to segregate." He watched as she did a quick exam from the horse's side.

"Baby's heart rate is strong and steady. Mother's is shakier considering her condition. Let's get her moved, get her in a clean area and we'll start a care regimen right away." She stood up, jotted notes into her phone, then faced him. "I won't pretend I'm holding out a lot of hope."

"Because she's so far gone."

"That and an almost full-term pregnancy puts a significant strain on the mother. How old is she?"

"Twenty-six." He didn't have to stop and think because he hadn't stopped thinking about Gingersnap—her formal name—since the day they hauled her away, twenty-one years ago. He'd been nine years old and had just witnessed what no child should ever have to see, the loss of his cousin and best friend.

And then he experienced the loss of another dear friend when they sent the horse to be euthanized. Nearly every moment since had been timed from that fateful day. Alfie gone, and Gingersnap hauled away to her death.

Only here she was, so someone else must have realized the horse wasn't at fault.

He didn't know how this happened, but seeing his old friend neglected and starved, he knew it was long past time to fix things. Starting today. "I'll get the trailer now that the others have loaded."

"Is your daughter strong enough to handle this?" She jutted her chin toward the group of watchful teens.

"My niece, actually. And yes. She's quite strong. Why?"

"Watching animals die is no picnic. And you and I both know this one's on shaky ground."

Regardless he still had to try. "We'll do our best and leave the rest in God's hands."

Doubt clouded her features. "Whoever left the fate of these animals to God didn't give them much of a fighting chance, did they?"

He faced her, calm and cool, and made sure she understood exactly what he wanted to say. "He brought them here, where they're surrounded by helping hands. I'd say He's done all right."

She didn't argue with him, but her expression indicated she wasn't buying into his reasoning.

No matter.

He needed her help. She needed work. They didn't have to get along or be friends, but when she murmured soft words of encouragement as they moved the mare forward, he wondered how someone so innately gifted with horses could be that far removed from God?

That was her business. Not his. And he would have enough on his plate once people realized that he'd just gone against a two-decades-old death sentence. A sentence that had never been carried out. A sentence decreed against a horse who hadn't done one thing wrong.

God had given him the chance to fix an old mistake. One way or another he was going to make up as much of that error as he could, and that would depend on how long Ginger and her baby lived.

Chapter Two

Isaiah Woods' ranch was about the prettiest thing Char had ever seen, and that was saying something for a girl raised on an elite Kentucky horse farm.

She drove her van beneath a wooden arch that read Dancing Meadows and was pretty sure she'd taken a step back in time. An L-shaped rustic log cabin stood to her right, shaded by towering pines. Wind chimes hung from the braces connecting the wooden porch pillars. They jangled a mix of sounds into the afternoon breeze as sunlight bathed the western side of the house. The natural light deepened the golden tones of the wooden logs. The whole thing created a suitable-for-framing Western-ranch image. As she followed the graveled drive to a system of pristine barns, she angled the van to the left and then paused.

Three meadows spread out behind the barns. Two lay fairly flat, with an occasional dip and roll. The third went up a hill toward the deepening forest that served as the backdrop to this beautiful landholding. But it wasn't the pretty green pastures that brought her to a stop.

It was the amazing array of colorful Appaloosas that made Char catch her breath.

Grays. Chestnuts. Buckskins. Blues. It was like viewing her favorite childhood poem, the one Corrie would sing to her, lulling a busy girl to sleep with promises of a new day coming. *Hushabye. Don't you cry... Go to sleep, little lady... When you wake, you shall have all the pretty little horses.*

Her heart went tight, remembering. Corrie Satterly had cared for all three of the Fitzgerald girls, from the time her oldest sister, Lizzie, was a baby. She had surrounded Lizzie, Melonie and Char with faith, hope and love. And yet... despite Char's love for her surrogate mother... it never seemed to be enough. Someday she'd have to take some time and figure out why. But not today.

"You like our horses?"

She turned, surprised.

A copper-haired boy faced her, and then he hopped up on the fence and pointed. "See that blue roan?"

There were several, but she saw the one he meant right off. "With the wider blanket." To the right a gorgeous horse stood slightly apart. The blue-gray coloration faded as it reached the horse's back, then merged with a wide blanket of pale cream, lightly speckled. "She's a stunner."

"She's named after me. Liam's Little Lady because we were born on the same day. Only I'm eight and she's four."

"A birthday present."

His eyes shined when he looked at her. "Yes, that's right. And I remember my daddy holding me up and saying, 'Well, then, what do you think, boy?'"

"And what did you think?" asked Char.

"I thought we would be like that forever." His voice went soft. He stared out at the horses as if suddenly watching a different kind of scene. "All of us here, with Uncle Isaiah, eating rice pudding and raising horses."

Sadness wound through his words, enough to keep Char from asking questions.

"Doctor?" The teen girl—he'd called her J.J. at the Armbrusters'—came their way from a service barn. A big red-gold dog trotted alongside her, ears up, tail wagging. A family kind of dog, happy and healthy. "We're over here."

Char indicated the passenger seat to the boy. "Want a lift?"

The boy shook his head. "Uncle Isaiah says if you can walk it, walk it. And if you can run it? Better yet." He dashed off in the direction of the older barn.

Wise words.

Char followed, then pulled the van near the broad, open doors facing the driveway. In a time when many old barns were in a state of neglect, this one wore its age with dignity. Three extra-large stalls lined the western wall, while neatly stacked hay and straw did the same on the opposite side.

"You came straight over."

Oh, that voice. His voice.

It drew her, but it wasn't just his voice. There was something else. Something in the firm, strong way he stood. His quiet demeanor. No excessive movements, as if simple stoicism meant more than meaningless activity. She didn't mention that she hurried this way because Ginger's prognosis was the trickiest. He already knew that. "I wanted to see her settled."

He led her to a big stall. The floor was thick with clean yellow straw. The chestnut roan was snatching hay from a wall-mounted hayrack. Nearby a clean water trough was full. A broad Dutch door faced the outdoors. The top half of the door stood open, bathing the stall in fresh air and light, while the bottom half of the door was firmly latched.

"Hey, pretty."

Ginger perked her left ear when Char spoke, but kept right on eating.

"I hate to interrupt the first solid meal she's had in who knows how long."

Caring. Kind. A man of conviction. Not exactly the kind of man she was used to. Was that her fault? Or theirs?

"Can we put off the testing for a day?" he continued.

She faced Isaiah as the two kids came into the barn. J.J. came their way. Liam hung back, close to the haystacks. The dog sat by his feet, quietly watching the scene unfold.

"My thoughts exactly. Let's let her get her bearings, and we'll run tests tomorrow. Right now good hay, fresh water and a clean stall are her best friends, and you've taken care of that."

"That was all J.J." He settled that look of pride on the girl again. "She's my right-hand gal with horses and she's already determined that Ginger's going to make it."

Char could write the girl a list of reasons why the horse probably wouldn't make it, but they'd face those hurdles in the days to come. "I like a solid optimist," Char told her as she extended her hand to the girl. "Especially when optimism is paired with a good work ethic. I'll come by first thing in the morning and take some samples. In the meantime I want to do a general deworming and start a course of antibiotics for whatever is causing that runny nose and cough. We'll go more specific if needed when we have the test results."

"Shouldn't she have a bath?" asked J.J. "I think she'd feel better after one, don't you?"

"She'd look better to us, but for her comfort's sake, let's just worry about food, water and the cleanliness of her surroundings right now. I promise you if this works, she'll look a lot better four weeks down the road."

"I hope so," said the boy.

He sounded worried. And when she shifted her gaze to him, his expression showed deep concern.

"She looks sad to be in here," he explained. "All cooped up with scratches and things when all the pretty horses are out there."

All the pretty horses. There it was again, from a child's lips, a phrase from that beloved poem. "She can't be near our horses right now, Liam." Isaiah squatted to the boy's level. "She's sick and she might make them sick. That's why we've got to keep her over here for now, okay?"

"Like when Grandma puts me in time-out?"

"No," said Isaiah kindly. "This is more like being in the hospital. Separated so we can give her time to get well again."

"If you'd behave yourself, you wouldn't be put in time-out," noted J.J., sounding so much like Char's big sisters that Char had to add her piece.

"We all outgrow time-out, Liam."

He lifted his brows, encouraged, and Char smiled at him. "It's part of growing up. Do you help with the horses?"

Another look of disappointment darkened his face. "I want to but Grandma says I'm too quick and they're quicker yet."

"He helps with chickens over at Grandma and Grandpa's house, up the road."

"They smell," Liam told her. "Like, really bad."

"Especially during rainy times," Char noted.

The boy wrinkled his nose and nodded as she administered the first dose of antibiotic. Then she offered Ginger a quick dose of dewormer.

"We had turkeys on our horse farm down south," she explained. "It was a thing with my grandfather, to give turkeys as gifts in November. And in those long, hot and humid days of summer, tending the turkeys was not a whole lot of fun."

Liam smiled when she flashed him a look of

commiseration. "When is her baby due?" he asked. "Like soon?"

"Pretty soon. I can't tell exactly, but I'd say sooner rather than later." She finished the parasite application and tucked the empty vial back into her pocket. "We'll do some measurements tomorrow."

"Then I'll skip camp and stay here to help," J.J. declared.

Isaiah's face stayed calm, but his voice pitched down. "Jodie June, I do believe we've discussed this."

"You discussed it by telling me what to do, but you know this changes things, Uncle Isaiah," the girl insisted. "She needs someone checking on her and caring for her. She's got to be more important than equine camp, isn't she?"

"Except the camp is paid for and you made a commitment. And we don't take commitments lightly. But the horse does raise a significant problem these next few weeks." Isaiah turned toward Char. "J.J.'s gone during the day and I'm knee-deep in work with hay and oats, on top of caring for our herds and dealing with scheduled visits of potential buyers. I can install a mare camera in here, but with her deterioration she shouldn't be left without regular supervision. Would it be possible to hire your services for the next few weeks, between your other patients? Stop over here, supervise her care, make sure we're not missing something vital because we're busy?"

Char knew how easily that could happen during crunch time on a farm or ranch. "I'd be happy to."

He didn't smile, but he did look relieved. "Good. J.J., can you go check the pasture troughs for me?"

The girl gave a reluctant look to Ginger, but nodded as she moved toward the broad door. "Sure. I'll make sure they're clean, too."

"I'd appreciate it."

"Hey, Rising." J.J. motioned to the big red dog. "Wanna come?"

The dog trotted after her, clearly at home. The slight swagger to his movements suggested his importance to the farm and this family. "Pretty dog."

"That's Rising," Liam told her. "He was my dad's dog."

"Rising, huh?" She aimed a quizzical look at Liam. "How'd he get such a cool name?"

"Red Moon Rising," said Isaiah. "My brother picked the puppy out of a litter up in McCall, and that night he saw a red moon rising so he used an old custom of integrating nature into the name."

"But you don't call him 'Red,' which would

have been most people's choice of a call name, wouldn't it?"

"Probably. Andrew got the dog to round out our family, and he saw the dog and the horses and this growing farm as a new hope rising. So that's why we started calling him 'Rising' and it stuck."

It wasn't just a good reason to nickname the dog. It was a great one.

Isaiah had turned back toward the boy. "And, Liam, how was summer school today?"

The boy's face answered that clearly.

"That bad, huh?"

"I don't know why I have to go to stupid summer school when almost everybody else in the whole world has vacation. I think Grandma just wants me out of the way."

"Liam—"

"I think you know it, too," the boy went on, "because little boys are too busy, too noisy and too pesky."

"Are you?" asked Char.

"Am I what?"

"Too busy, noisy and pesky?"

He frowned. "Sometimes. I guess. I just don't like being alone mostly."

Oh, she understood that kind of a problem too well. "So the good side of summer school is not being alone. The bad side is that it's school, right?"

"Half days. Then lunch. Then nothing but me stuck at Grandma's. With the chickens." He shoved his two little hands into his pocket and trudged off, the image of a lonely child.

"Ouch."

Isaiah winced, watching him.

"So, Isaiah." She was probably going to regret what she was about to do, and she went right ahead and did it, anyway.

"Yes?"

"Here's the plan. You do whatever is needed first thing in the morning. Text me an update. Then I'll come around late morning and hang out. What time does his bus bring him back?"

He followed her gaze toward Liam. "You mean Liam?"

"Yes."

"No bus, we carpool with one of the other families whose kids take summer classes. He gets dropped off at eleven fifty, but he'll be with my mother, up the road. And she's not going to let him come down here and help you. Not at his age."

"So, your mother is his guardian?"

That question got his full attention. "No. I am."

"Then as his guardian, why not bring him over here for the afternoons?"

"It's complicated."

"Only if you make it complicated," she supposed. She walked toward her van as she spoke. "A simple 'yes' could make it quite easy. He'd be company for me and out of Grandma's hair."

His face went tight. "My mother loves Liam."

"Even though he's busy, noisy and pesky."

She knew she hit a nerve when his eyes narrowed.

"Just a thought," she told Isaiah as she climbed in and started the van. "He's obviously lonely and sad and wishes life was different. I thought a change of pace might be good for him." She pulled away, but when she glanced into the rearview mirror, he was standing there. Not watching her. Not watching anything, really. Just standing there, looking as sad as the little red-haired boy now sitting quietly on the beautiful front porch.

So, she thought changing things up with his mother would be easy?

Dealing with his mother was never simple. Stella Woods was a stubborn personality, from tough Native American roots, and when it came to children, she drew a firm line. Especially with boys.

That realization cost him sleep that night.

She was tougher on Liam than J.J. He'd

chalked that up to maturity, but the veterinarian's words were a wake-up call.

Liam wasn't a happy child. He didn't act out. He didn't pester others. He loved to ask questions, and Isaiah liked answering questions, so that worked out well. But there was clearly a problem with the boy's current situation. Unhappy in school. Unhappy at his grandmother's. Unhappy with summer.

He climbed out of bed early the next morning. J.J. was already up and at the barn, checking on Ginger. The stall was freshened up. So was the hay and the water trough. She was inside the stall with the emaciated horse, whispering encouragement while she ran a gentle brush over the horse's body. "You beat me here."

She flashed him a resigned smile. "I wanted some time with her before Mrs. Rodriguez picks me up. I know I need to go to camp." She kept her voice soft as she stroked the horse's side and back with the soft bristles. "But I don't want to leave her alone."

"I'll be close by for the next few hours. And I got the camera installed last night." He motioned to the inter-barn system they used to monitor pregnant mares in the big barns. "I can keep an eye on her even if I'm not right here. And the doctor's coming later this morning."

"I'm glad she wasn't afraid to try to help the horses after Dr. Hirsch wanted them all put down."

"You heard that?"

"Yes. So did Brian and Jamie and Alex."

Her three best friends on the planet, and they all liked to talk, especially when it came to anything equine-related. "Professionals don't always agree on things," he reminded her. "And she seems to realize this is a dicey business for all of these horses, but for Ginger in particular."

"Well, I like her. She's not afraid to speak her mind."

J.J. was right about that, but Isaiah wasn't stupid. Going against Braden would have repercussions that could ripple across the tightly knit horse community and make things difficult for the new veterinarian. Braden had friends on ranches and farms, and a few in high places, and he wouldn't be afraid to use them.

He was also close with Isaiah's parents. He'd grown up next door to Isaiah's mother. Their families did everything together. On top of that, he knew everything about Ginger. Before too long Isaiah's parents would realize he was helping an old foe. And there would be reckoning.

His reckoning. And theirs.

He owed the horse. From the moment he realized who was lying in that field, he understood his need to face the guilt of the past.

A text from the veterinarian buzzed in. He opened it as he went back to the house to get Liam to school. How's she doing?

Holding her own, he texted back. Still eating and drinking. All functions appear to be working.

Good. ETA eleven.

I'll monitor until then.

A thumbs-up emoji came back to him. He put away the phone and smiled.

He stopped smiling when he spotted Liam's face smooshed against the front window, as if dreading the day.

Should he be forced to go to summer school? Was third-grade reading readiness that important? What if he was just a late bloomer?

How many battlefronts can you maintain at once?

Isaiah heard his grandfather's voice in the mental question.

Adam "Gray Cloud" Woods knew people even better than he knew horses, and no one knew horses better than him. He died too young— Isaiah could use a dose of that aged wisdom right about now.

"Do I have to go, Uncle Isaiah?"

The fact that Liam didn't cry, whine or carry on should have made the decision to say yes easier.

The opposite was true because a healthy, happy boy might have raised a ruckus about being shipped off to the three-week program geared to help students who were struggling in school. His quiet resignation showed how unhappy he was.

Would he mess up Liam's future by keeping him home? Keeping him here? Was he tempted to baby the boy because he'd been orphaned over two years before and still seemed to be floundering?

Yes. Which meant he should send him. "Not much longer, pal. Then you'll have almost a month of summer vacation left."

Liam said nothing.

Chin down, he got up from his seat at the broad kitchen island and picked up his backpack.

"Do you have your snack?"

A quiet nod. Then the boy walked slowly to the car.

Silent sadness.

The very worst kind, Isaiah realized as he climbed into the driver's seat. The kind that wore a person down like water on rock. It could either smooth out rough edges or turn the rock into sand. Which was it doing to his brother's precious son? He longed for the former, but something inside of Isaiah sensed that the boy's hopes and dreams were being withered away, and he wasn't at all sure what to do about it.

Chapter Three

"So, you've managed to rile up the horse community, insult the local veterinary surgeon and tackle an impossible task in less than forty-eight hours." Melonie Fitzgerald Middleton raised a coffee mug in mock salute to Char when the three sisters gathered in the Pine Ridge Ranch kitchen early that morning. "Well done. Even I didn't ruffle that many Idaho feathers my first forty-eight hours in town. It might be a Fitzgerald record."

Charlotte poured a mug of coffee and frowned. "I blame Lizzie. She read Ty Carrington's text about the horses and called me instantly. Totally her fault. I could have stayed in the stable apartment and been clueless. And blameless."

"Feel free to thank me, dearest, because you did the right thing." Lizzie looped an arm around Char's shoulders and hugged her. "While Braden Hirsch has been the go-to man for decades, he's not up on the newest things in horse care, and we need someone well-schooled in current findings. Uncle Sean put a lot of money and love into our equine barns, and I want solid medicine on my side. Which means I'm hoping you'll stay, little sister."

Lizzie had taken over management of their late uncle's fledgling horse-breeding business, an amazing enterprise modeled after the choicest Irish horse farms. While the girls' father had squandered his wealth and position in Kentucky, Uncle Sean had come north to make his own way in the world. And he'd done well. Char had moved into the apartment above the horse stables when she arrived. Lizzie had lived there before she married Heath Caufield, her old love and the farm manager. Then Mel had occupied the two-room living space until she fell head over heels in love with Jace Middleton and his two baby nieces. Now it was Char's place to call home while she tested the Western Idaho waters.

"Heath and I are thrilled to have you on board, Char. This could be the perfect opportunity for you. God's opened a big door, ready for you to shine."

"Or some horrible person neglected a crowd

of lovely animals and I was in the right place at the right time," Char mused. She sent Lizzie a wry look. "Science refuses to bear out your lofty celestial ideas, sis. But I respect your right to have them."

"Didn't DNA testing recently indicate that all men are related to one man? One single man from way back when?" asked Melonie. "That's gotta count for something, Char, when science proves the book of Genesis to be correct."

"Darlings, I love you." Melonie and Lizzie had both taken their coffees to the angled breakfast bar separating the wide kitchen from the equally wide dining room. "But it's too early to be throwing down this kind of talk—although you're both praying women—so I'd appreciate it if you prayed for these horses. It's a sad and sorry bunch they are, and I'd like to meet the person who let them get into this kind of shape."

"It's heartbreaking, for sure. And you said one of them is in foal?"

"An old mare with local history and a sad face. But she perked right up when she heard Isaiah Woods talking." Char sipped her coffee as she double-checked her leather bag. "Like one of those old-time reunion stories that make great movies."

"I love those movies." Melonie put a hand to her heart.

"Me, too," added Lizzie. "But I think talk time is over," she said as Corrie brought Ava and Annie their way. "Zeke never sleeps long once Mel brings the girls over for Corrie to watch."

"I'm ducking out quickly, then," said Char. "I'll play with them when I get home tonight, but if I hang around, I'll never want to leave, and duty calls."

"Go in peace." Lizzie paused and gave Char a big hug. "I love you. I'm so glad you're here."

"Me, too." Melonie reached up for a hug as Char went by. "See you tonight. And I'll be praying, Char. For you and the horses."

"I'll take all the help I can get." Char began her rounds up near McCall to check out the horse Young Eagle took home. Then she came back south, ran by the Carrington Ranch and then on to the horse-rescue farm just south of Council. When she finished she had just enough time to get back to Dancing Meadows. She pulled into the drive, parked and opened up the sliding side door of the mobile clinic. She didn't look around for Isaiah. She was here to see the horse. Nothing more. But when she spotted him coming her way, her heart jumped, so she tamped it right back down before he reached the barn.

"Right on time."

She carried a small tray of supplies into the barn and set it next to Ginger's stall. "I like being punctual, but I may have driven somewhat too quickly on that last stretch. I should have realized that curvy, winding mountain roads slow one's pace."

"And there's no such thing as a New York minute in Idaho."

"Well, I'm a blend of Old South and New York, busy so I've become my own conundrum," she admitted. "We'll see if I can reconcile the polar opposites here in the Great Northwest. Oh, sweet thing." She moved into the horse's stall with a sigh. "You look unhappy."

The horse blew out a breath. Her eyes watered, and then she stomped her back left foot twice before reaching around with her head toward her belly.

"Bellyache." Isaiah folded his arms like he'd done the day before. "Did we overfeed her, or is there something else going on?"

"With a horse in her condition, there could be a lot of things going on," she told him honestly. "We'll start with simple fixes first. Her digestive tract is oversensitive because of what she's been through, so let's change things up. No hay right now. We can walk her for five minutes every couple of hours. That way she grazes on fresh grass, but not too much. We'll keep the water in her trough on the tepid side to prevent cold-water cramping. The fresh grass will help reactivate the stomach so the intestines can do their job."

"I should have thought of that, but J.J. was out here early to take care of her."

"And no parent wants to discourage industry like that."

A horn tooted softly in the distance. "That will be Liam. I had them drop him here and I texted my mother that I'm going to keep him the next few days."

"Oh, good," she said, approving. "He can walk her with me. And maybe show me around? If you don't mind."

"He'd love it. He loves the horses and the ranch. He is truly his father's son, but my mother gets nervous about boys and horses."

"Not girls? Isn't that a little backward in the Wild West?"

"She finds girls to be more levelheaded."

Char aimed a skeptical look his way. "Clearly she's never frequented the suburban stables back east. There is an overpopulation of not-so-level-headed girls at some of the loftier places."

"Not exactly *National Velvet*?"

"No, but that was one of my favorite horse books as a child." The thought made her smile as she took samples from the horse's nostril once she'd drawn blood. "I grew up thriving on horse stories. The classics and the not-so-classics. When I wasn't reading about horses, I was living with them. Given that, in some ways I had the world's most idyllic childhood for a horse-lover."

"So, you were raised with horses?" he asked while she slipped the samples into a mailing sleeve. "That explains the natural affinity I see."

"My grandfather started a Kentucky horse farm when he became successful. He and my father bred racehorses," she told him. "Great-grandpa, too, but I never knew him. He died shortly after emigrating from Ireland. They loved horses. Maybe too much, in some ways, but yes, there's something in the blood. A predisposition that made becoming a big-animal vet a no-brainer. Equine doors tended to open quickly in the South and East when your last name is Fitzgerald."

Fitzgerald.

No.

Could this situation possibly get any worse than it already was? It just did.

She dropped the name as he was leaving, giving him plenty of time to think it over while he went up the gravel trail to the house to intercept Liam.

Was it a coincidence?

Most likely not.

Was she related to Sean Fitzgerald, one of the men who took advantage of the hard times nearly thirty years back and bought up Idaho ranchland when it was dirt cheap? Land that included his mother's family farm when her parents were strapped for cash three decades back.

Now the Fitzgerald holdings were valued in the millions, and all because Sean Fitzgerald staked a claim at the right time. But between his ranch, the Hardaway Ranch and Carrington Ranch, outsiders had come in and purchased multiple parcels of land as they became available. Some Native American land. And Middleton land, too, from another old homesteader's family.

Her van had only offered initials. CMF. But it couldn't be a coincidence that she bore the last name Fitzgerald.

"I can't believe I get to be with you today, Uncle Isaiah!" Liam had already ditched his school clothes, donned ranch clothing and sprang out the door like a meteor on a clear night. "How's the horse doing? Can I see her? Is the doctor lady here?"

She was here, but she couldn't stay. His parents weren't the only ones bearing grudges about those land deals. Thirty years later it was still a "what if" in many roundtable discussions.

And yet she had to stay.

With Braden's stance on Ginger, the new veterinarian had to oversee the mare's care. There was absolutely no other option.

"What's wrong?" Liam gripped Isaiah's hand. "Are you okay?"

"I'm fine." He wasn't, but he'd pretend for the moment. When they drew close to the barn, Liam sprinted ahead. "Hey! Doctor lady!" he shouted.

Charlotte turned and put a hand up, palm out. "Rule number one. We use inside voices around horses. Their hearing is sensitive and we don't want to upset or rile them."

"Is that why they have such big triangle ears?" he asked in a much softer voice.

"To hear predators coming. Yes. Horses instinctively listen, all the time. Our job is to keep our voices soft and nonthreatening. And you don't have to call me doctor lady. Just call me Char. All right?"

"Yes, ma'am." The boy aimed a sincere look her way. "I can be loud someplace else. Okay?"

"Perfect." She smiled down at him. "For right now I need you to be my gofer."

Liam made a sour face. "Uncle Isaiah doesn't

like gophers. Not one little bit. They make tunnels that trip horses."

"Ah." She raised her gaze and aimed it straight at Isaiah. And then she smiled and he stood right there, wishing she didn't. Wishing the smile didn't draw him in. Make him want to smile back and maybe keep smiling. "Well, I can see how that would be problematic with so many beautiful horses. But you're going to be a different kind of gopher, more like an assistant to me. When I need something, you run and get it. When I have questions, you answer them."

"Like about Uncle Isaiah? And the ranch?"

"Exactly like that. And you will be the official guardian of my bag." She kept brushing the mare in gentle, sweeping motions, as if she had nothing better to do than brush a horse. "That bag has all my emergency supplies in it, so if we have an emergency, you need to know exactly where the bag is."

"Like carry it everywhere?" he asked, eyes wide.

"Nope. No sense in that, is there? Not if we know where it is."

He grinned. "You're smart!"

"I agree." She smiled down at him, looked up, then paused, gazing over Isaiah's shoulder. Her eyes went still. The hand moving the brush faltered slightly, and her pretty smile faded just enough for Isaiah to turn around.

His mother stood ten paces back. Her expression said she was ready to do battle. He braced his legs and folded his arms, because if Stella Woods had a gripe with anyone, it was with him. Not the beautiful veterinary surgeon who was trying to establish a much-needed new business.

And not the softhearted little boy whose smile had disappeared the moment he spotted his grandmother coming their way.

Stella glared as she strode forward.

He met her halfway. "You come in peace for a poor neglected animal, I hope."

"What are you doing, Isaiah Michael?" she hissed, and he hoped Liam couldn't hear the venom in her voice. "You know better than to give shelter to a mean horse." She uttered a bad phrase in her native tongue, a phrase he'd never heard come out of her mouth before. "She has already taken a life from us, one that was precious and good. Now we should let her give up her spirit and be done with it. Isaiah, I'm begging you." She clasped his arms with her hands and gripped hard. "Do not save a murdering horse. It cannot be done."

It would be so much easier to play along.

He'd stayed quiet all these years, knowing the

truth and realizing there was little a child could do to change things.

But he was a child no longer, and God had put this opportunity in his path. Only a soulless man would shrug off this chance. "We would condemn a beautiful creature because of an accident, Mother?"

Her brow drew down. "A thrown child is no accident."

And here it was, the moment he'd been destined to face for twenty-one long years. "But a horse spooked by careless humans may react. And then the blame lies not with the animal, but with the person who knew better."

Her mouth dropped open.

She stared at him. Her eyes went wide before they narrowed in stark anger. "You cast blame with your words, Isaiah."

"Then I apologize because there is no blame intended, Mother." He hoped his tone offered assurance. "Accidents happen. We understand that. But it was wrong to lay blame on an innocent horse. It's been twenty-one years. The horse is sick and old. We should care for her the way you did for my grandfather in his time." She'd taken good care of Gray Cloud and set a beautiful example of how one should treat the aged. But his words didn't seem to hit their mark.

She stared at him.

Then the horse and Charlotte and the boy.

And then she scraped her feet against the stony drive, spinning fine gray dust into the air. "If you do this thing, I shake the dust of your existence from my feet. You can no longer be a child of mine. It is either the horse or your mother, Isaiah. There is no room for both in your heart."

And there it was.

The ultimatum. An ultimatum she'd made to others when angry. He'd heard it several times over the years and now it was his turn. And because she was a grudge holder, it was a promise he knew she'd keep. "But there is room." He stepped forward, hoping for a compromise with the woman who had borne him. The mother who had raised him. She loved him and loved these children. An enforced separation wasn't good for him, but it would be especially hard on Andrew's two kids. "My heart has room for both. It's time to let the truth set us free. Especially for her." He indicated the horse with a slight nod.

"You are young and foolish and wrong." Exasperation hiked her voice. "You think you see, but you do not, and your actions bring grief and harm to so many. Do as you will." She threw her hands into the air. "From this day forward you mean nothing to me."

"Grandma?"

She'd raised her voice on purpose. Liam heard. And Charlotte must have heard, too.

Stella ignored the longing in the boy's voice and stomped away.

"Grandma!" Liam began to dart her way.

Isaiah caught him up and held him close. "Let her go, Liam. She's angry right now. We'll give her time, okay?"

"But why is she mad? Is she mad at me? Again?" He buried his face against Isaiah's shoulder. His body shook but no tears came.

And when Isaiah raised his gaze to Charlotte, she looked from him to his mother and back as if the whole thing caused her way too much pain.

And then she quietly went back to brushing the poor, neglected horse.

Chapter Four

Char's phone signaled a text from Lizzie as Isaiah's Jeep headed to a far pasture a little later. Can you stop at the Council market for milk, bread and ice cream? And chocolate?

She texted Lizzie back once she'd rechecked Ginger's vitals. Tell Cookie I'm on it.

Bob Cook, aka "Cookie," managed the kitchen at Pine Ridge Ranch. "Although I'm pretty sure the chocolate isn't for Cookie."

Lizzie sent back a wide-smile emoji that made Char smile in return.

She hadn't lived with or near her sisters in a lot of years. They'd followed separate career paths until their father's embezzlement toppled the publishing business. That had cost Lizzie and Melonie their jobs this past year, and left Mel and Char with huge student loans to repay. Student loans were exempt from the bankruptcy rulings, so inheriting a share of Uncle Sean's ranch would help each of them get back on solid ground.

Char had gone her own way as she worked through her undergrad degree in Kentucky and then veterinary school at Cornell. She'd focused on her goals. Her future. Her dreams.

Now the sisters weren't just reunited. They were linked by Sean's bequest. He knew he was dying, and when he realized that his brother had left three daughters in dire straits, he'd written the sisters into his will.

The future of Pine Ridge was linked to the future of the struggling town nearby, Shepherd's Crossing. Lizzie and Heath had dived in to run Pine Ridge the way her uncle had hoped, with Heath managing the sheep-farm enterprise, while Lizzie took charge of the highly regarded horse stables. Heath's first wife had passed away from a heart condition exacerbated by pregnancy. His son Zeke had survived. But he and Lizzie loved each other and the ranch, cementing their roots firmly into the rich Idaho soil.

Melonie and her husband, Jace, were in the thick of remodeling a huge, neglected ranch house belonging to his biological grandmother. It was a mammoth project, and the newlyweds had been awarded custody of his twin nieces by their young mother...which meant Melonie had gone from single to married with a big job and twin tiny souls counting on her, two of the cutest baby girls in the world, Ava and Annie.

And now Char had arrived to fulfill her part of the bequest, to spend a year at the ranch, helping maintain it in light of Sean's demise. After witnessing a few over-the-top local reactions, she might have to rethink her idea of setting up a practice here to be near her sisters. A veterinarian needed steady work. If she got blacklisted for being on the wrong side of local issues, she'd have little choice. But that was a decision for a later day.

Liam had been sitting on a nearby stack of hay. She motioned him over. "Let's walk this beauty on fresh grass, all right?"

"I can come?" He leaped from the hay in one bound.

"If you can walk smoothly and slowly, with no sudden movements and a gentle voice, then sure."

"I can."

Such a sober face for a youngster. Shouldn't a little boy be flying kites and racing bikes over bumpy trails or catching frogs at the creek? Although it was probably a little dry for the frogs this time of year, making them harder to spot and catch.

She released the latch on Ginger's door.

Liam stepped through.

He gazed around at the stall, then the horse, then the stall again. And then he smiled.

Oh, that smile…

As if he'd just been handed a prize-winning ticket. He didn't wait to be asked. He moved forward, unlatched the lower half of the Dutch door and drew it open, then followed Char and Ginger out onto the grass.

The horse didn't hesitate.

Nose down, she browsed without moving too far from the door, and when the allotted time was up, Char was tempted to just let her go but she knew better. "Come on, girl. Back in for a while. We'll take another stroll later."

Ginger had other ideas.

She turned her head away from the lead and kept on eating.

Char gave an encouraging chirp to urge her forward.

Ginger ignored her. And just when Char was ruing her decision to bring the horse out of the spacious pen to help clear the bellyache, Liam moved closer. "Can I try?"

Little Boy Trampled by Irate Horse.

She used to make up headlines with Grandpa Fitzgerald when she was quite small. The old-time newspaperman had taught her how to turn any situation into a one-line summation, and it was an art she'd perfected over the years. "Liam, it might not be…"

The boy lifted his chin. He locked eyes with her. And then he reached up, stroked the horse's dark face and didn't reach for the lead. "Come on, pretty girl. Come along. There's more grass waiting later. Come along."

Liam stroked her face one last time, then moved toward the stable door.

And the horse followed him.

Char stood watching, mouth agape.

"Did I just see what I think I saw?"

She turned quickly. She hadn't seen Isaiah come back around. Hadn't heard him, either, and when she saw the dark chestnut quarter horse tied to the far rail, she knew why. "She followed him like a puppy."

Ginger went fully into the stall with no balking.

Liam stroked her face, told her she was a good girl, then slipped out the far side. He looked up when Char and Isaiah came in through the nearby door. "She likes me."

No denying that. Char nodded. "She does. She liked your voice, and how you handled her and how you let her decide."

"I like those things, too."

"To make your own decisions?" asked Isaiah.

"Some, anyway." Liam lifted one shoulder. "It's never fun when everyone is your boss."

"I hear you." Char tucked her medical bag into the van before she came back toward them. "I was the youngest, and between my sisters and my nanny and my grandparents, I was bossed around every night and every day it seemed. Until I learned that if I just took a horse out and spent a day roaming, no one would bother me at all."

"Like by yourself?" Liam asked and she saw the light in his eyes right off.

"Not until I was older than you are right now," she told him in a firm voice. "At your age, we buddy ride. Although I'd be open to giving any of those guys a workout as needed," she told Isaiah as she motioned toward the horses at pasture. "What an amazing herd. How do you keep them exercised properly?"

"It's tough this time of year," he admitted. "My father and I are double-teaming the second cutting of hay. We just harvested winter wheat, so we'll be baling straw tomorrow. And I've got buyers coming in from Utah this week." He seemed on the verge of offering her an invitation to ride, but he didn't make an offer, and she was foolish to want one when there were several horses to ride at Pine Ridge. "Do you have disinfectant for boots and shoes between barns?" That was a proper doctor-patient question. "Ginger might not be contagious, but if she is, you don't want it back there."

"Agreed. And yes, I filled the disinfectant trough yesterday. I'll change it up regularly. The only two between here and there will be me and J.J."

Isaiah's face was in profile to Liam. He didn't see the boy's look of longing.

Char did. She bent low. "Do you know what Isaiah is saying?"

He glanced down, guilty, and shook his head.

"Ginger's runny nose might be contagious. It could make the other horses sick, so there's a special pan in the back barn for rinsing boots. Just like this one." She pointed out the disinfectant pan not far from Ginger's pen. "It kills germs."

"So we don't get sick."

"Most germs that hurt horses don't hurt humans."

That spiked his interest. "Why not?"

"They don't like us. But those germs like horses a lot and they can make them super sick. So Uncle Isaiah has these special soaps to keep the germs from getting back there." She pointed to the back pastures.

"I won't go back there. I promise. Not without Uncle Isaiah."

"Thank you, little buddy." Isaiah looped an arm around his shoulders. "I've got to go fix a broken belt on the baler. You want to tag along?" he asked the boy.

Liam's face lit up. "Yes!" He sloshed his rubber boots in the trough, then started for the equipment barn.

"Hands, too, Liam. Germs are tiny, but they're all over the place."

"But there aren't any horses in that barn." The dark red metal barn stood off to the side, and the gleam of well-kept equipment was apparent from this angle.

"But if we take germs to that barn, and then someone goes to the horse pasture…"

Liam slapped a hand to his forehead. "Then the germs go to the horses!"

"Exactly."

Liam didn't just wash his hands. He scrubbed them while Isaiah checked the mare-cam settings and alarm system. When the boy was done, he used the heavy-duty paper towels to dry them. He waited until Isaiah motioned, then he hurried to his side. He reached up.

Isaiah reached down.

Their hands clasped, and the sight of the big, dark-haired cowboy and the red-haired little boy didn't just touch her heart. It grabbed hold and wouldn't let go. His love for the boy and Liam's love for him…

She'd craved that feeling for so long. The love of a father figure, like so many of her friends had enjoyed. Seeing it between Isaiah and Liam satisfied her. She'd read the longing in Liam's eyes the previous day. They moved off, but then Isaiah looked back as they curved along the gravel drive. He didn't nod. Didn't say anything. Didn't tip the brim of his tan cowboy hat. He simply met her gaze for long, slow seconds.

Strong. Caring. Quiet.

She'd read fictional stories about kind, nurturing men, but hadn't come across all that many in real life. And when she did, they were either married or old enough to be her grandfather.

Isaiah was neither, but the last thing she needed or wanted was more family drama, and Dancing Meadows had a lion's share of it. Been there. Done that. Overrated.

She went back to Ginger and cooed soft words to the emaciated mare. And when it was time to take the horse for another turn around on fresh grass, she attached the lead and opened the door.

A lot of horses in this condition would have stormed the door, anxious for food.

Not this one.

Ginger plodded along, and as they moved into the greener area, she huffed a breath, reached out and laid her equine cheek against Char's shoulder in a gesture of trust.

Char paused. She reached up and stroked the horse's face and neck, murmuring words of comfort. And when she looked up, over the horse's downturned nose, Isaiah was watching from the equipment shed. Was he watching her? Or the horse?

Both, she decided.

He smiled.

Not at the horse. At her. And although she knew she shouldn't, she held his gaze across the long drive. And then she smiled back.

"How is Ginger doing?" J.J. bounded to the truck as soon as Isaiah pulled into the riding-academy loop later that afternoon. "Is she hanging in there? Did she deliver?"

"Yes and no and you can see for yourself in a few minutes," he told her as she scrambled into the passenger side of the front seat.

"I got to help walk her," announced Liam from the back seat. "Char let me open the doors and we walked her around the grass and let her eat. And then we let her rest. And then eat again. I think I would be like so bored if that's all I had to do," he finished.

"We've got to take things slow so we don't make her sicker," J.J. told him. She turned back to Isaiah. "What did Char say? What did she do? And aren't you glad to have a new young doctor around that wants to try new things with horses?"

Isaiah treaded lightly. "New things have their place, but there's a reason our people developed an amazing line of horses, J.J. Because they listened with their ears and watched with their eyes and learned from their experiences. They bred for specific qualities long before there were animal doctors on the scene."

"Well, Char's grandpa and great-grandpa were horse breeders. Big ones. In Kentucky." J.J. spoke in quick, short spurts as she munched a handful of trail mix and held up her phone for him to see. Except he was driving and figured paying attention to the road was more important than whatever app she'd stumbled on.

"Did you stalk her online?"

"It's not stalking when all you have to do is put the Fitzgerald name in, and boy, did a lot come up. Not so much about her," she went on when he sent a surprised look her way. "But her family. Her dad's supposed to be in prison, Isaiah. Not the local lockup like you get for running over Grady Bursten's prize roses."

"Well, they did win the blue ribbon at last

year's Western Idaho Fair." He grinned her way. "Grady was mighty proud of those flowers, and Billy Warbler was their total undoing."

"Well, this was big stuff with Char's dad," she told him, and she stressed the word *big*. "Millions of dollars, not a few twenty-dollar bushes. He took the money and ran off overseas. And they all had to declare bankruptcy, the publishing business and the family."

Isaiah didn't ask what happened to the three daughters.

He'd just figured that part out. That explained why Sean Fitzgerald had bequeathed his sprawling ranch to the three nieces. Sean had been a man of valor. Clearly his brother—the women's father—was not. Now all three were here, in Adams County. "She seems to know her stuff." He turned into their drive as he spoke. He didn't add that it was a good thing because he was pretty sure Braden wouldn't be passing a peace pipe anytime soon. Could her veterinary business survive with three clients? Him. The Carringtons, owners of Carrington Acres neighboring the Fitzgerald spread. And Pine Ridge? Probably not. "That's what matters."

"Do you think Ginger will be all right?" J.J. posed the question when he rolled to a stop not far from the back door of the log house. "Does she have a good chance?"

He wasn't about to get J.J.'s hopes up. She and her brother had gone through enough disappointment. "I can't say. Pregnancy puts a major strain on the body, but the doctor says there's a shot. So we take that shot and see what happens."

"Can I go straight down?" J.J. set her gear on the back porch and jumped the rail. She landed softly in the grass below. "I can help with dishes after."

"I'm not one to refuse an offer of help like that. You take the evening shift. I'll bring supper down and load the dishes. Take your brother with you." When she started to frown, he folded his arms.

The frown disappeared. "I will. You guys were teaching me all kinds of things at his age. Come on, Liam." She called to him as she crossed the drive. "Wanna help with Ginger?"

"Yes!" He didn't shout.

That was Char's influence and it was a good one.

He watched them go as he ignited the propane grill. He'd have preferred a wood fire, but there wasn't time to build a fire, tend it, make supper, care for the animals and raise the kids.

Propane was easy, but it gave him time to consider J.J.'s words. *You guys were teaching me...*

They'd been a unit then. Him. Andrew. His

sister-in-law, Katie, and the kids. His father and Gray Cloud talking, planning, seeing to the business of redeveloping the best Nez Percé horses they could with help and advice from his veterinarian godfather. They'd shared chores and dreams.

Then Gray Cloud passed away and Andrew and Katie were lost in a late-night crash on their way back from a friend's wedding, obscuring hopes and dreams in the ashes of grief.

But now—

A horse whinnied from the broodmare barn. He looked up and saw his father and Braden and Braden's brother exiting the barn. Steven Hirsch was their representative in the state legislature. He had a small spread with half a dozen horses closer to Boise.

Two paths diverged from the pastoral setting. One came toward the home he'd built five years before. The other veered southeast toward his parents' place. The men took that path, and not one of them looked his way.

Funny how the very thing that gave him hope was the thing that divided their family. A horse, given a second chance. A chance others would have denied her.

Fortunately it wasn't their decision, but being sequestered from his family stung. They'd already been through the wringer. Was he making it better or worse with his actions?

He wasn't sure but the thought of standing by while Braden put Ginger down stung deeper. The humans involved had options. The horse was at the mercy of those choices, and in all situations Isaiah ranked compassion first.

When the burgers were done, he made a plate of three sandwiches, a bowl of chips and a pitcher of lemonade.

They ate in the old barn, with the aged horse, and when the kids were done eating, no one whined about chores or work or their day. How could they when they sat in the company of a sorely neglected animal? An animal who never uttered a peep of dismay.

When they'd put their stuff away, J.J. let Liam take lead, walking the mare. She snapped a few pictures of them together, then sent them off with a few strokes of her thumbs. "Are you sending those to the kids at camp?" he asked when she pocketed the phone.

She shook her head. "To Char. I want her to see how well Ginger's doing. And she'll be happy to see Liam leading her."

It *would* make her happy, he realized.

Why did that matter?

It shouldn't, he scolded himself as the kids walked Ginger around the fenced-in paddock.

He was already knee-deep in muck with family. Welcoming a Fitzgerald into the realm would only make things worse.

But her opinion did matter. Maybe because she pointed out what he should have seen. That Liam needed a chance to spread his wings. To be a boy.

It shouldn't have taken the words of a stranger to make him see that, but it had. And when that stranger texted back a happy-face emoji, J.J. held it up for him to see. "She's proud of us! And she says we should leave the top Dutch door open tonight. There's a nearly full moon and horses love the moon."

They did.

His did, anyway. And most folks didn't know that about horses. That the extra light brought out the best in them.

"She says the Idaho moon is good, but the Kentucky moon is better."

He grinned.

"The farther south you go," J.J. kept reading, "the closer you are to heaven."

"And closer to Mom and Dad!" Liam punched the air. "I knew horses were smart. I knew it!"

Isaiah's heart melted with the boy's earnest words. What a wretched thing to have life changed up so utterly and completely, with nothing to be done about it.

Isaiah roughed up the boy's carrot-toned hair. "The horses have nothing on you, kid."

Liam made a skeptical face. "I don't think smart kids go to summer school."

"Sure they do," countered Isaiah. "Because they want to stay smart. You'll be done in two weeks and you can practice your reading with me over August. All right?"

"And I'll read to her." Liam watched as Ginger rubbed against the walls of the big stall. "And her baby. I can come down here and sit on the fence and tell them stories about lots of things."

"I expect they'd like that."

The thought of reading to the horses made Liam smile, and that smile eased another pang of worry from Isaiah's shoulders. Liam had smiled more today than he had in the last month.

Was that because of the horse, the spunky veterinarian or just being allowed to be a boy—moving, running, jumping?

Maybe all three, but it didn't matter. The only thing that mattered was seeing both his nephew and the horse safe. He was okay with that.

Chapter Five

"The Adams County Rodeo is coming up and I promised Zeke we'd go." Lizzie spooned food into little Ava's mouth while Corrie fed her identical twin, Annie. "We should all go." She looked up at Char, then Melonie. "It's good to support local efforts and I love the change of pace of rodeo."

Melonie had horse issues from an accident years before, but she agreed as she made fresh coffee. "I'll do anything for Zeke-man," she told them. "If I go into duck-and-cover mode, don't be surprised. But rodeo food is enough to make me say yes. Fried dough?" She pretended to swoon. "Be still my heart!"

"Aren't you supposed to be at Gilda's now?" Gilda's house was the big renovation that brought Melonie and Jace together the month before. Char looked at the clock. "It's nearly nine."

"I'm consulting on a new project today, on Main Street in Shepherd's Crossing," Melonie replied. "They're remodeling an old building into a professional office space and asked me to meet with them. A spark of life for our quiet village."

The little town could use Melonie's help. The number of closed businesses and empty houses didn't bode well for the locals. "Is this where they steal your ideas, make them their own and pay you nothing?" asked Char as she packed two protein bars into her bag.

"You leave those suspicions back east, darling." Melonie hugged her, then kissed the babies one at a time. "Welcome to the West, Char. Where good men actually keep their word."

Char sent her a look of disbelief as Melonie hurried out the door. "Please tell me she doesn't really believe that?"

Lizzie scrunched her face. "I have to say I've seen it with my own eyes, so yes. She means it. And I think that double-wedding thing validated her claim." Melonie and Lizzie had shared a wonderful Western-barbecue Independence Day wedding, and spent their time grinning like newlyweds whenever their new husbands were around. It was absolutely wonderful and amazingly annoying all at once.

"Heath and Jace are good guys," Char agreed,

"but I'm not sure if that's the norm or just a fortunate turn because things couldn't go more downhill than they did last year."

"Things can always go more downhill, darling girl." Corrie kept her attention on the nearly one-year-old baby but her words were for Char. "And still we move forward. We strive, as the good Lord intended. Even if we shake our fist at the clouds from time to time."

"Corrie, I have known you every day of my twenty-six years." Char leaned down and kissed Corrie's soft brown cheek. "And I don't think you've ever shaken your fist at anything. It's one of the most amazing truths there is."

"I've done my share." This time Corrie looked up. "When unrighteousness hurts my girls, or when sin takes precedence over family, or greed interferes with the joys of life, I have made my feelings known to God in no uncertain terms. But telling him my feelings is different than blaming him for the weakness of men. Some are good. Some aren't. Our job is to bide our time until the right one comes along. And then to be open-minded enough to see."

"Wise as always. I'm off to do the rounds of the rescues. If by chance I get any calls on the ranch phone, can you give them my cell number?"

"Happy to do so," Lizzie told her. "And I don't

want you worried if it takes a while to build a client base here after that bust-up with Braden. You've got three horse owners who will gladly hire your services."

"Which I appreciate," Char replied as she slung her bag over her shoulder. "But starting off being blackballed wasn't exactly how I saw this going down. On the other hand, I do like a good fight."

"There is truth in those words," muttered Corrie, and Lizzie laughed.

"I'll keep spreading the word. And if I weasel out time to get a weekly newspaper going, we can do a feature article on the new mobile veterinary service in town. My goal is to start with a Labor Day edition and go from there."

"That's six weeks away. Can you pull that off?"

Corrie snorted and Char grinned because this was Lizzie, and Lizzie never let anything stand in her way. "I retract my foolish question. You're a Fitzgerald and it's publishing. In this case the two are inseparable."

"Horses and news. And pretty girls." Corrie rubbed her forehead to Annie's and the little girl laughed out loud. "Time marches on."

It did, Char agreed as she started the van a few minutes later. Her life had taken an abrupt one-eighty, and she'd been so upset by that...

Well, that and the lying, scheming boyfriend who tried to implicate her in his underhanded horse trading back in Central New York. A scheme that cost him his chance at a veterinary license and a huge fine.

Suspicion and doubt had become her new mantra. If people wanted her trust, they had to earn it. And even then she would proceed with caution, so why did she want to throw caution to the wind the minute she spotted Isaiah coming her way a few hours later?

Ridiculous.

But it didn't feel ridiculous when he looped his arms around the top fence rail and watched her work with Ginger. "For a horse in her condition, she seems strangely content," he told her. His hands rested lightly on the rail. He seemed at ease, even though the horse's presence had messed up his life. Was he that accustomed to a messed-up life? Or was he immune to drama?

That was an idea she could adopt straight-out, but she kept her attention on the horse. "Has this always been her nature? Or is she just happy to be loved and cared for after her recent neglect?"

"Maybe both." He frowned slightly and she fought the urge to smooth that frown. "I was young when she was sent away, but I loved her. And that day, one single day, everything went wrong. And it never really got right again."

"But you're fixing it now."

His dark eyes rested on the horse. Sorrow filled his gaze. "Mending what I can. But when you tear the heart of a fabric, even the best mending is still a patch job."

"There was a time when tires weren't replaced," she told him. "They were patched. And when a bone breaks and heals, the broken spot is actually stronger than the bone surrounding it in most cases. So a patch isn't necessarily a bad thing. It's just a thing."

He smiled.

When he did, her heart melted on the spot. Did he sense her catch her breath? Hold his gaze a little too long?

"Good analogy. You're right, and I'm not melancholy. I just wish people could admit their mistakes and move on. It would make things so much easier."

"Pride and fear get in the way. And sometimes greed. Selfishness."

"Your father."

She winced, then shrugged. "That was a bad deal, but it wasn't exactly a huge surprise. My grandparents and great-grandparents built the publishing empire. They were true entrepreneurs with an ear for the business of news. My uncle Sean opted out when he was young, after a stint in the service. He got the farming genes and he did well. Sometimes I wonder if my grandparents dreaded handing the business over to my father. If they sensed the writing on the wall. But once they were gone, it didn't matter."

"It mattered to you." Isaiah's voice gentled. "And your sisters. What should ever be more important than the children around us?"

"You have lovely priorities," she told him as she noted Ginger's vitals into her tablet. "That's not the norm in my experience."

"I'm sorry for that, little lady."

He sounded sorry and the quaint phrase touched her, as did the sympathy in his voice. As if her feelings and her isolation mattered. "Old news." She finished up and flashed him a smile. "I'll take her for a walk. I'm sure you've got things to do."

He'd folded his arms loosely on the rail, leaning in, classic cowboy. And then he didn't move. Didn't shift his gaze. He kept those big brown eyes right on her as if standing there was more important than anything on his to-do list. And for just a moment, she felt important.

He sighed and pushed back. "Too right. Liam and I are going to meet prospective buyers from Utah in an hour."

"Do you sell a lot of horses?" she asked and he shook his head.

"Not many yet—we're just getting to that

phase," he told her. "We used to run cattle and there are still sixty head on Dad's land east of here, but my brother and I decided to develop the Appaloosa line when we were teens. We worked, scraped together money and worked some more. We bought horses, grew hay, developed brood stock, and then raised and broke the foals. It's been ten years in the making and we've got fourteen pregnant mares in the back field. Six up close, sooner to deliver and eight around back. Do you want to come see them?"

Of course she did, but she'd been with the rescues all morning. She shook her head. "I'll accept the invite when Ginger's better and we have confirmation that we're not tracking some horrific virus out to them. I know we're all disinfecting, and if there was a medical need I'd chance it, but why risk such a huge and wonderful investment of time and resources?"

He wanted to talk her into it.

Which was silly because she was right, they'd be foolish to risk contaminating his livestock. But something about her drew him.

Yet he couldn't be drawn. He'd already alienated family over the horse. To throw a Fitzgerald into the mix would add salt to the wound, and it wasn't as if his parents hadn't suffered enough by losing their son and daughter-in-law.

He took the Jeep to the back barn and when Liam joined him a quarter hour later, the boy had changed out of his school clothes, made his own PB&J sandwich and was wearing his farm boots—with socks. All good things.

His phone buzzed a text from Char. I'm here for a while. Does Liam want to hang out with me?

He posed the question to Liam. "Char's wondering if you want to hang out with her and help with Ginger."

"Yes!"

Isaiah understood the boy's enthusiasm because he wanted to hang out with her himself. Good looks and great figure aside, her strength called to him. And something else, too. The more-fragile side, the side that made her raise her defenses. He caught it in her stance and sometimes in her eyes. She hid it well, but it was there. A hint of suspicion, as if self-protection was the rule. Not the exception.

"Head over—she's waving."

Liam jumped off the rail, but he didn't run straight off. Instead he turned and grabbed his uncle in a big hug. "I love being over here with you, Uncle Isaiah." The boy whispered the words into Isaiah's shirt. "It's so much better."

He was gone in a flash, but his words lingered. He'd let his mother watch Liam for both their sakes, he'd thought. He thought watching Liam would relieve his mother's grief at losing the boy's father. And that Liam would be safe and sound in the grace of loving grandparents.

His mother's tight rein had stifled the boy. Why hadn't he seen that more clearly?

He had, he realized.

He just hadn't wanted to make waves over it, and that was his fault. Being a peacemaker was good to a point. But there were times when even a man of peace had to stand strong and take one for the team. Char's comments made him see that.

A wide-bodied pickup rolled in a few minutes later, pulling a four-horse trailer.

He and Andrew used to dream about cutting big deals. They'd sold a few horses each year, but this year was the beginning of the culmination. This year all the hopes and dreams came together with multiple buyers showing interest in their tribute Appaloosas. It was an honor he should be sharing with his brother and Katie.

Now he'd do it alone.

He strode forward and extended a hand, and when MacLaren Farms pulled away with three mares and a gelding two-and-a-half hours later, he brought up his bank account on his phone and whistled lightly.

A year's pay in one short afternoon.

It should have felt good. It should have felt wonderful, but his brain flooded with other should-have-beens.

Andrew should have been here.

Katie would have baked a cake and used cream-cheese frosting to make it special. And they'd throw steaks on a wood fire and take a few hours to celebrate their dream before jumping in all over again.

"They bought four horses!" Liam was running his way. The dog loped behind him at a more measured pace.

When Liam reached him, he hurled himself into Isaiah's arms. "Who has so much money that they can buy four horses, Uncle Isaiah? It's like a lot of money, isn't it?"

He grinned and hugged the boy. "It is a lot of money."

Char was waiting farther down the graveled drive. He walked her way, still holding the boy, who was really too big to be held. And yet it felt right.

She slid her gaze toward the ranch exit and smiled. "Congratulations."

"Appreciated. And having Liam busy with

you was great. Thank you." He set the boy down. "How's Ginger doing?"

"She seems quiet this afternoon. Off her feed."

"Labor?"

"Maybe. Or maybe just getting her body re-accustomed to regular meals. We'll keep a close eye."

"Which means you should have supper with us tonight." He didn't plan to invite her, but the minute the words were out of his mouth, he was glad he did. "To celebrate the first major sale and to keep an eye on an old friend. I'll grab steaks out of the freezer before I leave to pick up J.J."

"How about we go get J.J. so you can get afternoon chores done?" she suggested. "You can keep an eye on the mare cam, but that way you're not an hour behind. And there's nothing for Liam and me to do with Ginger right now."

"You wouldn't mind?"

"Not at all," she told him. "I love that J.J. picks my brain for information. She's one horse-savvy kid."

"Grandma says she's just like Dad." Something in Liam's voice cued Isaiah to listen more closely. "That she's like Dad in a girl's body."

His mother often compared the children to each other, and their family. J.J. didn't care, mostly because she was going to do her own thing in any case.

Liam was more sensitive. He wanted to be like his dad, but his dad was gone.

Isaiah bent low. "When I see you making plans for the day, every day, it's like seeing your dad all over again."

"Really?" Two red brows shot up.

"Your dad always planned his work to get it done first so the rest of the day was his."

"I do that all the time!"

"Exactly like your dad."

A grin split Liam's face. Isaiah sent him toward the house. "Make a pit stop in the bathroom before you head out with Char. And then you can help with dinner when you get back."

"Okay!"

Liam ran off. The dog followed. Isaiah turned back to Char in time to see her dash a tear away. "Wait. What?" He stared at her, then the boy, then her again. "I don't do tears. Like ever. So stop that. Now."

She laughed at his deliberately overdone panic. "I expect you're fine with tears and/or anything else, Isaiah Woods." She swiped her hand to her cheek one more time. "I came a little undone seeing Liam's reaction. How much he loves you and loves this ranch. These horses. It's like he's blossoming before our eyes."

She'd described it perfectly and he gave her shoulder a gentle nudge with his. "Well, you laid down a challenge and made me see that I could fix things if I stood my ground."

"My sisters will be pleased that my snarky nature has reaped a reward," she bantered back. Then she softened her smile. "It's good to see kids happy."

"The best."

Liam chased back to them and Char hooked a thumb. "You've got shotgun until we pick up your sister…and then you're in the middle."

"But—"

"Seniority, kid." She winked at Isaiah as Liam scrambled into the van. "There's always a pecking order. That's how life goes. Now's as good a time as any to learn that lesson."

She climbed into the driver's seat.

It looked right, seeing the boy beside her. Seeing his bright eyes, hearing him laugh. As if it was meant to be this way.

She paused as she thrust the van into gear. Then she glanced back at him.

Was she thinking the same thing? That this felt too right to be wrong?

She drew a breath. A breath that made her narrow shoulders rise, then fall.

And then she pulled away, but not until she'd angled one last look his way, as if wondering…

A look that made him feel really good inside.

Chapter Six

When the van disappeared from sight, he didn't go straight to the afternoon chores.

He hooked a right turn toward a small hollow that lay east of his house. Two simple wooden crosses flanked a gray marble marker bearing two names. To the right of the names, a climbing rose marked Katie's love for gardens. On the left the artist had etched a series of pine trees behind a single beautiful horse.

Katie and Andrew's ashes had been put here. And he'd helped his father lay out a resting nook edged in bright green grass and a garden, curved like a crescent moon.

Andrew had always loved the crescent moon.

He stood there, eyes down, praying silently. He was proud of their successes. Proud of today. But it wasn't his success alone that turned this corner, and his heart ached, wishing Katie and Andrew were here to be part of it.

But they that wait upon the LORD shall renew their strength; they shall mount up with wings as eagles; they shall run, and not be weary; they shall walk, and not faint.

He read the verse from *Isaiah* inscribed on the beautiful headstone.

Andrew's favorite. He used to joke that his little brother got a whole book of the Bible and he got about a dozen mentions.

But then he'd loop an arm around Isaiah's shoulders, give him a noogie and say Isaiah got the best book of all: the old prophet, a sayer of truths.

"I miss him."

John Woods's voice startled Isaiah. He brushed a hand to his eyes and turned toward his father. "Me, too."

"I saw that trailer pulling away, fully loaded. A deal like that doesn't come every day."

"No, it doesn't. And we should all be here to celebrate it." He pondered the stone and those two simple crosses. "But we won't be." He turned toward his dad. "I'm cooking steaks in a couple of hours. Would you and Mom like to join us?"

His father frowned. "She won't come any-where near you or that horse right now. And she's pretty sure that new doctor is here to mess up everything."

"You don't believe that." His father had to deal with Stella on a daily basis, but John Woods was a practical man.

"Of course not. I think Braden has been resting on his laurels for a while. He's taken with the idea of being the only game in town. In the whole region, actually." His father leaned his arms on the split-rail fencing bordering the memorial garden. "Competition pushes excellence. When there is no competition, it's easy to get complacent, and there's no place for complacency on a ranch. Not if you want it to be successful." He turned and leaned back against the rail. "Isaiah."

And here it was, his father's plea for peace. To mend things. To capitulate to keep his mother happy.

But his father surprised him.

"You're doing a good thing. A fine thing. Saving that horse is what we should do to fix a wrong that's gone unfixed for way too long."

Isaiah stared at him as realization dawned. "You know what happened that day?"

His father made a face. "I didn't. Not for a long time, but I do now. And it's a grievous thing for a person to carry that guilt all these years and try to cover it up. It's not healthy and

I told your mother that, but she's dug a hole so deep, she can't see her way out. The truth might seem harsh, but it can set her free."

His father knew of his mother's part in Alfie's death. "She didn't mean to scare the horse."

"Of course she didn't. She was impetuous. She was always that way and it was one thing I've always loved about her. She made a mistake, one she's been paying for over twenty years. But she needs to come to terms with it. And she never should have asked for your silence, son. She put too much on a boy's shoulders and I've told her so." He gazed toward Isaiah's place. "The truth will come out now. As it should. And I don't want you or my grandkids caught in the crosshairs."

With the horse in his barn and a Fitzgerald giving veterinary care? Isaiah didn't try to mask his skepticism. "I'm not sure that's possible."

"It would be more possible if your mother came forward." John frowned. "That's my prayer. For her to take responsibility and nip this anger. Loose talk grows like a storm in the mountains. Quick, fierce and destructive. Braden was quick to malign the new doctor to anyone and everyone who would listen. More Fitzgeralds coming in, changing things, taking over."

So they knew Char was a Fitzgerald, and

Braden was laying groundwork to mess up her chance at success. "She's a veterinarian with solid horse expertise. That should be the bottom line."

"It should be. But fear and guilt make people do stupid things. Regardless." His father faced him squarely. "I'm on your side. And I'll help any way I can."

"But, Mom—"

"There are no buts, son. There's right and there's wrong, and the wrong's been going on for far too long. It's time things got put right."

And when John hugged Isaiah, it wasn't just a hug. It was a benediction.

Most of the Nimiipuu wanted to live in peace. But their tribal history was important. Their heritage and legacy with the Appaloosas was nothing to be forgotten, and they'd lost a great deal to power-hungry people over a century before.

Isaiah had no intention of letting that happen again. His ranch, his horses, his choices. Nothing should narrow tribal options for the future but Braden liked his sense of power. He always had. Was he looking out for the greater good or his own pocketbook? The latter, Isaiah surmised.

I will fight no more forever.

Chief Joseph's words of wisdom, words Isa-

iah lived by, but now the fight was at his door.
A different fight, but a battle nonetheless.

"I'm proud of you, son. What's more—" his
father jutted his clean-shaven chin toward the
memorial "—they'd be proud of you. Stand
tall and righteous, like you've always done and
things will work out."

His father headed back home.

So did Isaiah. J.J. helped with chores once
they returned, and by the time he came up front,
restlessness pushed him. He needed to start a
fire. Grab some rolls. Maybe pull some vege-
tables out of the freezer.

The ripe smell of smoke wafted to him as he
rounded the curve.

Thin gray plumes rose from the firepit. The
cooking grate had been laid across it. As he
drew closer, Liam came out of the log cabin. He
was carrying four plates. Char followed with
silverware. The pair proceeded to set the table
on the back porch as he approached.

His restlessness ebbed.

A different feeling stole over him, and when
Char looked up…

When their eyes met…

Longing stirred. An old longing, or maybe
brand-new, but when she smiled at him, those
old worries abated. He returned the smile as he
jogged up the steps. "You guys got stuff ready."

"It seemed outrageously rude to have you do all the farm chores while we sat around, waiting to be waited on, so I swung by Pine Ridge to raid the kitchen."

She didn't look guilty about her admission, and that deepened his smile.

"Cookie had just shopped, so I appropriated four big potatoes—"

"Idaho, of course."

"Top-notch, all the way." When her smile deepened, a dimple flashed in her left cheek. "They're roasting in the fire, and I hope it's okay that Corrie sent a luscious carrot cake with cream-cheese frosting. She'd baked several and donated one most happily."

Katie's habit of making a cake with cream-cheese frosting...

His heart picked up even more. "No, that's wonderful, Char. It's the perfect way to celebrate."

"J.J. told me it's a family tradition. So I thought a blend of old and new was in order. The new being my cheesy spoon bread, a totally Southern thing that is perfect next to a good steak."

The thought of blending old and new sounded good to him, and having her here seemed too right to be wrong, no matter what her last name was. "Char."

She turned from putting a hot pad on the table. Caught his eye. His gaze. Held it.

She brought one hand up to her throat, as if wondering.

So was he. She lowered her eyes as a faint blush crept into her cheeks, making him wish he could do more than wonder—but embroiling these two kids into whatever conflict might descend on them couldn't happen. Watching her with the kids, making them laugh, making them think, he wished it could.

And the amazingly delicious spoon bread only made the thought more desirable a quarter of an hour later. "This is amazing," he told her.

J.J. agreed. "Char, I could eat this stuff all night. It's like the best ever. How did you learn to cook like this and go to school and be a vet? Because I'm pretty sure veterinary school takes a lot of brains," the teen exclaimed.

"My nanny."

"Say what?" J.J. paused with a fork upraised.

Liam giggled. "Grown-ups have nannies?" He burst out laughing at the thought. When Char made a scolding face at him, the boy laughed harder.

"Corrie *was* my nanny," she explained. "And my substitute mom because my mom died when I was a baby."

Their smiles faded. They understood the reality of that too well.

"My dad was busy and we had no mom, but we had Corrie. And she has stayed by our side through everything. So even though I didn't have a mom, I had someone who loved me and taught me and raised me to be the best person I could be."

"Was it enough?" J.J. whispered the words in a tight, tiny voice as if a great deal depended on Char's answer.

"It was. Because in the end, love conquers all," she told them, but she didn't belabor the point. She helped herself to half a potato and a generous serving of sour cream. "We deal with the rough patches in life and we celebrate the good times, just like we're doing now. To you— all three of you." She lifted her glass in a toast. "Congratulations on a job well done."

They lifted their glasses and touched hers with a quiet clink, then drank.

Before the kids could go too deeply down memory lane, Isaiah changed the subject. "Ginger was holding her own?"

"Yes," Char answered smoothly, as if she knew what he was doing. "False alarm. Her wounds are healing nicely and we should have the lab report back sometime tomorrow."

"That fast?" asked J.J., and Char nodded.

"They'll email me so I can adjust meds if needed. It's amazing how quickly things can get done these days."

J.J. exchanged a look with Isaiah.

"What's going on?" Char paused her fork and raised a brow. "What did I miss?"

"Dr. Hirsch waits for reports to come back the old-fashioned way. It takes longer and gives us more time to worry about the horses."

J.J. had given Char the perfect opening to malign the older veterinarian.

She didn't take the shot.

She shrugged lightly. "Well, animals and vets have been doing that for a long time, and I expect he's saved a lot of discomfort and lives in his time. Speed can be helpful, but mostly it's tender loving care that gets things done."

"Unless a catastrophe hits." J.J. hunched forward, always eager to share horse knowledge. "Bitsy was telling us about how an epidemic shut down the big horse facility at U Penn's veterinary hospital and how they had to remodel the whole thing to make sure they killed the virus."

"A rarity," Char told her. "But something we guard against any time horses come together. And that sometimes depends on the honesty of people to keep a sick animal at home."

"Like the rodeo?" Liam asked.

Char nodded. "That's why they have vets on hand to check things out. Does Dr. Hirsch handle the veterinary care at the Adams County Rodeo?" she asked Isaiah.

"He does. And he's extremely careful because some folks get overzealous about competing and forget to put the horse's welfare first."

"Like winning is everything." J.J. directed her attention toward Ginger's barn. "It's not. Being good and kind and raising horses to be the best they can be. That's something."

"I don't mind winning," Char told her, and the frank note in her voice strengthened the words. "But I don't like winning at any cost. And that's the difference. Although some horses carry viruses within them and the owner has no idea until the virus activates for some reason. And now…" She pushed back her chair and stood. So did Isaiah. "While I should stay and help with dishes, I'm going to run over to the barn, give our friend a final look, then head home. I haven't had much time with my little nieces or nephew and I want to spend an hour with them before they're all tucked in bed."

"Can we come see Pine Ridge sometime?" asked Liam. "I've always wanted to see it, but Grandma said no."

"Did she?" Genuine surprise indicated Char had no inkling of the old feud. "Of course you can. Come see the sheep and the dogs and the horses. My uncle had just gotten a really cool quarter-horse stable up and running when he lost his battle with cancer, so my sister Lizzie has taken that on. If it's got anything to do with horses or publishing, Lizzie is our go-to gal."

"I'd love to see it," replied J.J.

What could Isaiah say that wouldn't sound downright dumb? That his family resented Sean Fitzgerald's success? That some of them were still fighting a war that should have been laid to rest long ago?

"Let's plan it for next week if all's well with Ginger. And my sisters are taking Zeke to the rodeo this weekend. Do you guys want to go?"

Liam nodded yes instantly. He swung toward Isaiah, imploringly. "Can I? If my chores are all done and I practice my reading?"

"Without being scolded into it?"

"Promise. Like cross my heart."

"I think we'd all like to go but Ginger will need watching if she hasn't delivered. And maybe if she has. You don't mind taking them?" he asked Char.

"It will be fun. I've never been to a rodeo and it will be good to sit on the sidelines and watch someone else do the work while I eat popcorn. Or fried dough. Please tell me they have all the really bad foods I love there."

"Guaranteed."

"Excellent!" She'd taken off the jaunty baseball hat she wore like second skin. She put it back on as she turned. "I'll see you guys tomorrow."

"Okay!" Liam's smile brightened his face. His eyes. His whole being.

"Can I come with you to check Ginger?" J.J. didn't wait to be invited. She hopped out of her chair and caught up with Char quickly. "I'll do dishes when I come back," she called over her shoulder.

He watched them stride off. One fair, one dark. Almost the same height. J.J.'s growth spurt last year had meant a lot of shopping.

She wasn't a kid anymore. She was a young lady with hopes and dreams and hormones running amok.

How did a single uncle raise a teenage girl?

He saw Char fake-punch J.J.'s arm for something the girl said, and when J.J. tipped her head back and laughed out loud, he sighed.

She needed a woman around. She loved his mother, but J.J. had well-honed people instincts and knew that his mother wasn't a confidante. She wasn't the kind of person you generally went to for advice or wisdom. What she lacked in empathy she made up for in work ethic, but that meant J.J. really didn't have another woman to talk to.

It appears she does.

He brushed off the mental reminder because as nice as Char was, she wouldn't be a constant once Ginger improved.

She could be.

He ignored the mental voice, cleared the dishes, then opened his laptop to record today's finances.

Little-boy laughter came through the front screen door. Liam was playing with Rising. He'd throw a tennis ball and Rising would not only run and get it, he'd chase back and drop it at Liam's feet. Then Liam would swipe the damp ball against his pants and throw it again. It was a sweet, normal dog-and-boy interaction that hadn't been the norm in a long time.

Today it was.

An engine started up. Char leaving. And when he heard the crunch of tires on gravel, he had to resist the urge to step onto the porch. Wave goodbye. And then he kicked himself for resisting the urge.

But they that wait upon the Lord...

The verse from *Isaiah* steadied him. He was generally a patient man. Maybe too patient at times.

Right now he needed that patience to give

things time to unfold. When he was around Char, patience was the last thing on his mind, and wasn't that an odd and sudden turn of events?

A horse whinnied from the back barn. Another joined in. Then all was quiet except for J.J.'s humming while she loaded the dishwasher and Liam's voice, encouraging the dog.

It all seemed so normal, as if an unexpected peace had stolen over Dancing Meadows in the fading light of a summer's day.

Right until three quick, successive gunshots cracked the air north of the house. J.J. jumped. Liam let out a little cry of surprise as Rising charged toward the meadow.

Liam shrieked for the dog.

Isaiah shouted, but the trusty dog flew up the gravel, guarding his family, disappearing into the shadows as they deepened. Then one more shot rang out.

And Rising stopped barking.

Chapter Seven

Char was headed north on Route 95 when J.J.'s number flashed on the Bluetooth display on her dashboard. She hit the button, heard the panic in the girl's voice and arced a U-turn that would have done a country boy proud.

"Someone shot Rising."

Fear knotted Char's throat. She swallowed it down. That dog…a beautiful, trustworthy animal, so loved.

"Uncle Isaiah is out there. We don't know who was shooting. Please come, Char. Please! Hurry!"

Char forced a professional calm she didn't feel. "I'm turning back down your road right now, J.J."

"What do I need to get for you? What do you need, Char?" Desperation marked the girl's voice, but she stayed steady enough to ask the right questions.

"I've got everything I need. Is Rising at the house or the barn?"

"Grandpa's place, two driveways up from us. East," she added, giving Char a clear idea. "I'll wait by the road and guide you in."

"Perfect."

The girl disconnected, and when Char passed Isaiah's house two minutes later, J.J. was visible up the road. She hopped in when Char paused, then pointed. "Grandpa's barn. It was the closest spot. Oh, Char, I don't know what we're going to do if we lose Rising. He was my dad's dog and…"

She didn't have to finish for Char to understand. Right now the beloved dog was a precious link to the parents they loved and lost. She spotted Liam as she steered the van around to open the surgery side toward the barn. The boy was perched on a rail post midway down the barn alley. Tear streaks marked his face. His hands were clenched. He looked at her.

Then the dog.

And in that look he begged her to make everything okay.

She didn't offer false hope. She couldn't offer words of encouragement. Not yet. She got out, opened the surgical side of the unit and within seconds Isaiah and a second man—Isaiah's father, from the look of him—had Rising on the stainless steel table.

The second man wasted no time. "I'm a tech, Doctor. You tell me what to get and I'll get it."

An extra pair of hands would be a wonderful thing. She did a cursory exam, then scrubbed up at her on-board sink. When she stepped away, the older man did the same.

The dog was in rough shape.

Major damage had been done to his back leg. He was going into shock and the partially open pant was split with an intermittent cry of pain.

She took care of the pain first, put the dog under with Isaiah's father's help, then tracked the bullet's path via wireless technology. "It went clean through, but we've got thoracic damage here." She pointed to the picture on the computer screen. "We need to go in, repair that and probably transfuse. Fortunately the bullet missed the heart and lungs."

"Whatever we need, Doctor." The older man's voice was both strong and weak. Then she found out why. "I did this to him when I was chasing off a pair of wolves snooping around our foaling barn. If anything happens to him…" Pain marked the man's face. "It's on me."

Tears streaked down Liam's cheeks freely

now. Because of the dog or because his grandfather had shot the dog?

Don't think.

Act.

She flipped the switch to professional mode.
The humidity had risen steadily through the
day. Sweat beaded across her forehead, then
slid toward her eyes.

"Char."

She looked up. Isaiah had folded a small,
clean towel. He blotted her forehead quickly
and gently, keeping her field of vision clear.
And then he did it again, as needed, while she
worked on one damaged site after another until
they were done a long time later.

"Can we move him to my house while he's
still under?" Isaiah asked as she stripped off the
disposable mask, gloves and gown, and then
deposited them in a bag-lined trash receptacle,
part of the surgical suite.

"This house is closer. Can he stay here?" she
asked before she caught sight of Isaiah's mother
across the barn.

Dark eyes bore into hers. Strong eyes, shad-
owed with animosity. A gaze that had been
forged from anger and loss, yet with an empti-
ness Char seemed to understand.

Isaiah's father started to speak, but Isaiah replied first. "My place is better right now."

Char did a mental count to ten, then decided she didn't have enough time to count high enough to tame her emotions. She stayed professional for his sake. And the kids'. And the poor dog. "I've got the stretcher inside." She motioned to Isaiah's dad. "If you bring it out, we can load him and transport him."

"And you'll tell me how to watch him overnight?" Isaiah pressed as his father withdrew the portable stretcher and unbound it.

"I'm spending the night," she replied as they positioned the rolling gurney to transport the beautiful retriever. "I want to monitor his progress and keep IV fluids going. If he throws a clot or anything goes wrong, I'll be here to intervene."

"So will I." Isaiah's father faced her. "It was a foolish mistake on my part, especially after such a good day for my son. Both sons," he acknowledged, and a sheen of tears made the man's light brown eyes reflect the lights around them. "I'll stay the night. Isaiah needs his rest, as do the children. The one responsible should always bear the weight of that responsibility."

The woman's quick intake of breath drew Char's attention. She shifted it back to the patient deliberately. They slid the gurney into the van's hold and clamped the restraints down. Then Char motioned to Isaiah. "Can you and

J.J. get us over there? Liam and I are going to ride in the back."

"Absolutely. Dad?" Isaiah opened the door as he turned. "There's room."

"I'll walk over."

Char took the boy's hand. He followed her willingly, and when he climbed into the back of the big van, tears filled his eyes again. He swiped the hem of his shirt up to his face and breathed in. Then he leaned down to the dog's face. "It'll be all right, Rising. You'll see, boy. It'll be all right. I promise."

And then the boy laid his head against the dog's side in a gentle move.

Tears spilled down his freckled cheeks, but he didn't say a word. He didn't sob or wail. He just lay there, giving the dog the best medicine ever. The prescription of love. And all Char could do was hope that her intervention and the family's love would be enough.

Pale hair.

Ivory cheeks.

In sleep, peace replaced the sadness Isaiah sensed in Char. The hinted longing, the struggle to do better, to be faster. Stronger.

Citius. Altius. Fortius.

Faster, higher, stronger, the Greek Olympic motto they'd adopted in high school track, when racing won him the scholarship he never used, because being here with the horses was enough. Now, recognizing how the world around him had narrowed, he wondered. Had he done enough? Or had he been complacent to accept less?

She stirred and brought one hand up toward her cheek, then dozed again.

Beautiful, thought Isaiah from the comfy, worn recliner. He'd let her sleep purposely. She'd scold him, because she'd made him promise to keep her on vigil with the dog, but when her eyes grew heavy…and her breathing leveled out…he vowed silently to keep watch as long as she needed.

The porch light slanted a beam of pale yellow across her hair. Long, golden locks splayed over her right shoulder, contrasting with the clean dark blue scrub she'd donned when Rising's surgery was over.

"She knows her stuff all right."

Isaiah's father whispered the words from the other side of the room.

"I've never seen a vet do so much in so little time," he went on. "As if instinct guided her hands."

His father had spent a dozen years working for Braden while building his cattle ranch on the side. Before that he'd worked for another veterinary practice that had closed up shop long ago. He'd watched the science of animal care change over the years and he didn't praise lightly.

"Rising wouldn't have made it with Braden," his father finished softly.

John was right.

Braden was good in many ways, but surgical skills on small animals weren't his forte. "We've got a ways to go still," Isaiah answered. He eased the recliner into an upright position and stood, stretching. "But she was pretty impressive."

Char's eyes blinked open when John stood to join Isaiah. She didn't have to glance around and reorient herself. Her attention went straight to Rising and the vitals. "You let me sleep. After I told you not to. And his vitals look good."

"My bad." Isaiah reached down and gave her a hand up. Once he had her hand in his, he didn't want to let it go. But he did, of course. "You sound surprised."

"Not surprised. But happy about the vitals. And relieved. We've got to avoid infection and that means we monitor closely."

The injured dog gave her another reason to be here.

You need a reason? Really?

He tabled that thought as she pulled her hair into a faded fabric band patterned with horses.

She saw his glance, then his expression, and put one hand to the band. "Occupational hazard. Corrie made these for me when I entered vet school. A dozen of them in different animal prints. The horse and dogs are my faves."

"Here you go." Isaiah's father handed Char a steaming mug of coffee. "Isaiah said you were a coffee drinker."

"Avid."

"With cream and sugar." Isaiah set the cream—real cream, not milk or half-and-half—next to the sugar bowl.

"One can never have too much sugar, regardless of what the magazines say. Thank you for letting me sleep," she told him, then included John in her look. "Did we ever get properly introduced, Mr. Woods?"

He shook his head. "John, please. And thank you for jumping in like you did, Doctor."

"Char," she reciprocated. "We'll see how it goes. I expect wolves have been causing problems?"

His dad snorted lightly. "To several area farms. Sheep. Goats. Calves. The government just came in and removed three from a pack that had gotten too accustomed to farm livestock. That sent the rest of their pack northward, or so they thought, but the two I saw tonight weren't heading anywhere. They were after a quick meal."

"The horses wouldn't let them near the colts and fillies, would they?"

"No." Isaiah agreed as he set his mug down next to hers and tried not to think how nice they looked together. "But a pair of wolves can cause some major damage to a horse or a colt, so why take the chance? Usually it's sheep they're bothering but the sheep farms aren't going into the hills like they used to. And if the food doesn't come to the wolf…"

"The wolf must come to the food."

"Exactly. They were chased off a couple of sheep farms the past few days."

"Clearly these two didn't get the memo about leaving livestock alone."

"That doesn't make my rash action any better, though." John studied his mug gravely. "I didn't wait until I had a clear visual, and the barking sounded like it was coming from behind, as if Rising was chasing a third wolf. And so I shot."

"The mountain plays games with sound some nights."

"I should have known better. It was a foolish mistake. An old-man mistake."

"Sixty isn't old, Dad." Isaiah rested a hand on his father's arm. "We all make mistakes. We own them, learn from them and go on. A smart guy taught me that," he added with a pointed look at his father. "Words he might want to take to heart."

His father's quiet gaze rested on the prone dog. "He's got to make it. I can't even think how it would affect the kids if—"

His voice choked. He went to sip his coffee, then held it there, midair, unmoving. Finally he set it down again without bringing it to his mouth.

"He's got a solid shot, John."

She didn't baby his father. Isaiah loved that because John Woods wouldn't appreciate being coddled. He faced his mistakes as needed, same as he'd taught his sons.

"But he's going to need some loving care for a while. I know it's a busy time here."

"Not too busy to care for an old friend," John told her.

She gave him a firm nod. "That's what I was hoping. Between you and your wife and Isaiah and the kids, I think you guys can handle this."

"You really think he'll make it?" This time John didn't watch the dog. He turned his attention to Char. She met his gaze full-on.

"I hope so. But if he doesn't, there are a lot of puppies and dogs looking for a place to call home. They might not have been your son's, but they're in need of love, the same as this guy was seven years ago. It would be sad to see that little boy without a dog at his side."

"Words to think on." He stood. "If it's all right, I'll take my coffee over to your spot on the floor. That way I can sit and pray and put it in God's hands."

"Where it should be," said Isaiah.

Char didn't agree.

She didn't disagree, but her silence said a lot. He caught a glimpse of the hinted loneliness he'd seen before. Just a glimpse.

His faith had been shaky once. He'd been full of himself and so sure he knew it all.

Andrew had laughed at him. He hadn't chided or scolded, but he'd laughed. And then led by example. And the year before he died, Isaiah had come to faith.

Not easily, of course.

There may have been some kicking and screaming on the way, but peace had eventually replaced that fruitless search for happiness. For joy.

His brother used to say, "Let go and let God."

Isaiah finally got the gist of that, and when that phone call came—the one no family ever wants to get—he wasn't the wayward twenty-something who was stuck on himself. He was a man. A man who now had two kids to raise.

"How is he?" J.J. tiptoed out of her room. She hurried to his father's side. "How's he doing, Grandpa?"

"Holding his own."

She curled up beside his father. John settled an arm around her shoulders. She laid her head against him, and the two of them sat, taking watch for an old friend.

Isaiah looked to his right.

Char wasn't watching the dog.

She was watching his father and J.J. with such an expression of longing that he wanted to reach out. Tug her close. Erase that look completely. Maybe forever.

Rising stirred. He gave a soft, piteous whine.

All business now, Char moved forward. She adjusted the meds slightly, then stepped back. "The sun's coming up. I'm going to give Ginger a quick look."

He was about to go with her when Liam hurried down the hall. "How is Rising? Is he okay? Is he all right?"

Isaiah lifted the boy and put a finger to his lips as Char slipped out the back door. "He's sleeping so his body can heal. We'll know soon, okay? For right now we have to be really quiet. And pray."

"I know." Liam's voice stayed somber. "I've been praying all night, mostly. I just don't want anything else to die. You know?"

Isaiah knew, but this wasn't up to him.

He looked toward his father.

John Woods sat quiet and still, with one arm wrapped around his beautiful granddaughter, and his gaze locked on the injured dog. His stoic profile said nothing of the struggle he must be feeling inside, but one lonely tear snaked a path down his father's cheek.

Brokenhearted by one foolish action.

The stoicism was real, something he'd taught his children, but that single tear said that it didn't come without pain.

Char had to get away.

Not from the dog. Performing emergency surgery on an injured animal was what she did best. The reason she went into mobile vet services was because she loved the crazy pace and the travel that comes with big-animal care, and most facilities weren't built to handle horses, cows, sheep and pigs.

That part was fine.

It was the absolutely selfless love that John Woods showed his grandchildren that grabbed hold of her heart and wouldn't let go.

The old ache wrenched open inside her.

Tears threatened.

She choked them back.

No one got to see her cry. Not even back when she had hoped and prayed and wished for a parent to love her...

Not when her boyfriend tried to make a scapegoat of her by using her sign-in accounts on the computer as he scammed horse lovers out of their pets...

And not now.

She strode into the old barn.

Ginger flicked her head up. When she spotted Char, she neighed softly. Then she nodded twice, blew out a breath and came toward Char in a gesture of pure trust. A gesture Char sorely needed right now. She reached out and hugged the horse as the soft tread of footsteps sounded behind her. She turned as Corrie slipped into the barn with a fresh cup of coffee and a wrapped breakfast sandwich that was layered with egg, bacon and cheese. That was Corrie. She didn't wait to be asked to help. She just did it, and it had been like that from the beginning.

"You eat this and keep up your strength," bossed Corrie as she came closer. "I can tend to this pretty lady. What needs doing?"

"Food. Water. Cleaning the stall. J.J. will come out to do it. I just wanted to check her out before I go back to the dog."

"Mmm-hmm." Corrie didn't buy it. She aimed a skeptical look at Char. "Let me say this, sweet thing." She placed two firm hands on broad hips once she set the food down. "You have not been able to fool me for a very long time, Charlotte Mary. Not since you were brought into this world as a tiny baby, this big." Corrie made a small basket with her arms. "I looked down at you and you looked up at me and we have loved one another ever since that day."

She was right. Char loved Corrie. Corrie had been there through thick and thin. She'd flown east last winter, when that whole debacle about selling horses hit the news. She'd stayed right there, too, until the truth came out and never uttered a word of reprimand or made Char feel stupid for trusting the wrong person.

"But I can also tell when things aren't quite right. And when things are just dreadfully wrong. And when that soul of yours gets to aching," she added softly. She moved into the stall, murmuring soft words of comfort to the mare. "An aching heart is nothing to be brushed off, pretty girl."

"Just tired. It's been a few long days," answered Char. She should have known Corrie wouldn't believe her.

"Life sends long days on a regular basis."

Corrie kept her voice low as she brushed the horse with sweeping, gentle strokes. "Doesn't matter where you're hanging your hat or what sort of business you're in. But that other look, the one you don't let most see. Well…" Corrie didn't look at Char. She didn't have to because she knew she was spot-on. "That's what concerns this old nanny."

"You're not old, Corrie."

Corrie laughed softly. "I'm on in years. I started this job with your mama when I was in my thirties. Life has a way of turning a body around and I found myself in unexpected circumstances. And then I met your mama and we took to one another right off. When she hired me to help raise her babies while she got drawn into business things, it was a marvelous opportunity, one I'd never sought nor expected."

"You weren't a nanny when Mom hired you?" Funny, Char had assumed that Corrie had come from an agency. It wasn't all that long ago, after all.

"I wasn't. But when she handed Miss Lizzie over to me, I realized that maybe there was a reason for it all. Why we met. How we met. And maybe God put me in the very place to soothe my soul when it most needed soothing."

Char had unwrapped the sandwich. The combined scents wrapped around her as guilt swept over her. "I shouldn't be out here eating while they're all inside, caring for the dog."

"No worries on that. I dropped a half dozen sandwiches there first. They told me you'd come down to the barn and I followed. If one of my babies is in trouble, that's where I need to be."

Total Corrie, showing them a love so kind. So true. She'd stepped into a void and filled it, so why did Char walk through life feeling abandoned?

She wasn't left with nothing or no one. She had a good life and Corrie's love. Why wasn't it enough?

"Stop fretting and eat your food while you tell me what in the name of all that's respectful in this world is going on with this poor neglected animal?" Corrie kept stroking the horse and kept her deep voice purposely soft. "I have never seen the like and I've been on the planet a long time. And she's about to have a baby, too. What a shame," Corrie added.

"We don't know what happened. Who had them. Or why they wandered in where they did."

"Well, horses are funny astute, aren't they?"

She meant they had an instinct for things, so Char nodded as she chewed. "They are."

"And they broke into a place where help waited."

Also true, so Char nodded.

"And you happened to be called in because you'd just arrived."

"Accidents of timing, Corrie. No more. No less."

Corrie kept her attention on the horse, but didn't look convinced. "Did you ever wonder why when things go well, we call it a coincidence, but when things go bad, folks blame God?"

"I don't wonder about that at all, actually."

A smile brightened Corrie's dark face. "You do, but you're not taken to admitting it, and it's always been that way with you. That's not a bad thing, sweetness. Asking questions, seeking answers—that's what slated you to be an animal doctor. You love helping and you search for answers. Two wonderful qualities."

"Whereas I thought I just loved working with animals and the rest followed along. This sandwich is amazing, by the way, and the coffee is, too. Thank you."

The change of subject wasn't lost on Corrie. She aimed a knowing look at Char, then resumed brushing. "God brought us here, child. All of us. Through the generosity of your uncle, yes, but it wasn't an accident. It was a blessing."

"I can't argue the blessing part. And we sure were blessed when you took us on, Corrie. I don't know what I'd do or where I'd be without you." She meant that sincerely. She had sought Corrie's gentle counsel and shelter during no small number of Fitzgerald storms.

"The feeling is mutual. How funny that the winding road brought us so far north, where things are different." Then she went on in that nice-and-easy Southern voice that meant she was making a point and you better listen. "But then there's folks, darlin'. And they're pretty much the same anywhere. We friend some and we take care around others because not all are as they should be."

Char had messed up before. That was then. This was now. "I'm less naive than I was last year."

"Less naive is good, but we still want to trust when we can. Find that balance. Who to believe. And when to take a chance as we go forward."

Char made a face when she finished chewing. "Trust is precious, Corrie. When it gets betrayed on a regular basis, we tend to keep it in short supply."

"Then we trust with care," Corrie told her, keeping her voice soft. "But we don't stop trusting."

Char didn't want to argue. She understood Corrie's point of view. The older woman wore her faith like armor and Char respected her. And loved her. Corrie had been with her through everything.

But the whole "faith of our fathers" thing wasn't on her agenda. She liked facts, not fiction, and trusting an intangible with no evidence went against the grain of an educated woman.

Does it? The insistent tiny voice niggled her brain. *Didn't your fancy schooling prove that something never comes from nothing? So why couldn't there be a God? Because everything you see, feel, hear or touch came from something, didn't it?*

She shoved the voice aside and drank the coffee. She was too tired to make sense of it, and both the horse and dog needed her attention.

"You come home to sleep tonight, all right?" Corrie directed that to Char, then stepped out of the stall as J.J. came into the barn. She flashed a smile at Isaiah's beautiful niece. "Your dog, your horse and your family are in my prayers, child. Such a nice spot you have here, built with love and devotion."

J.J. sighed as she moved toward the horse with a slower step than normal. "It's been a good place. A place where dreams were supposed to come true."

"And that's a thing about life," Corrie told her. "Dreams don't always come true on our timeline. But that doesn't mean they won't. Sometimes they're just different dreams. Ones we hadn't hardly thought of."

"Like saving this horse." J.J. ran her hands over the horse's neck and Ginger preened forward, enjoying the light touch. "I'm glad Uncle Isaiah brought her home. Saving her is a good thing to do."

"Exactly like that," Corrie agreed. "A major kindness like this doesn't just save a life. It teaches us to watch for opportunities to help. We keep our eyes wide-open and see what's put along our path."

"My mom used to say stuff like that." J.J. had reached for the grain bucket. She turned toward Corrie. "'Watch for opportunities, Jay,' she'd tell me. 'They're everywhere, but if you go through life focusing on yourself, you'll miss them. They're not all plain as day. Some are subtle, hiding in the shadows.'"

"Your mother and I would have gotten along fine," declared Corrie. "Just fine. Because sometimes it's the folks tucked in the margins of life we can do the most for. We just have to notice they exist.

"And now—" she crossed her arms and faced Char "—I must go. I promised Cookie I'd show him the proper way to make a Low-Country boil, which means I've got to grab a few things in Council."

Char may have only been in town for a few days, but she'd never tasted anything better than Bob Cook's barbecued ribs and dirty rice. Regardless, no one did Southern cooking like Corrie.

"That man is fine in the kitchen," Corrie continued. She lifted her bag, the kind of purse Southern ladies were known for. Small enough to be genteel, but big enough for an old-fashioned purse-whomping if needed. "But a boil isn't something you make fancy. It's good because it's not one bit fancy, and I was surprised a Western man like him didn't get that."

"I think he was trying to impress you, Corrie." Char recorded Ginger's vitals and meds in the electronic notebook. "Heath did say you're the first person Cookie's ever allowed to share his kitchen, and that's mighty big praise from an old-time cowboy, isn't it?"

"Or just plain smart, because a wise man knows good help when he sees it. You catch a nap today, okay?" She aimed a pointed look at Char and Char nodded.

"I will." When Corrie gathered her in for a hug before she left, it felt so natural and normal. But her life hadn't been either for a long time. Maybe ever.

Feeling sorry for yourself gets you nowhere. What is normal? And maybe normal isn't all

*it's cracked up to be. Maybe the normal you're
searching for is an illusion. Which means maybe
you're searching for the wrong things.*

She might be, Char realized, then capped the
thought with a yawn as the sound of Corrie's
car faded. "J.J., I'm going up to the house. I'm
staying here today, so if you want an update or
just want to talk, call me." She made a phone
symbol with her right hand. "I'll be right here."

"Thanks."

Char started to leave. Intuition made her
pause. Turn.

J.J.'s chin was down and her shoulders shook
slightly. But enough. Enough to know Char
couldn't walk away. "Jay?"

J.J. didn't turn, so Char moved forward. The
look of anguish on the teen's face didn't just
grab her heart. It tugged her soul. And the tears
slipping down J.J.'s face left her no choice.

"Oh, Jay." Char didn't think. She acted. Just
like Corrie would have done to her. She reached
out and took the teen into her arms and let her
have a good long cry. And when J.J. finally
stepped back, she swiped the sleeve of her T-
shirt to her face, mopping blindly while Char
grabbed a few pieces of somewhat dusty paper
towel from a nearby roll.

"Sorry."

"Oh, don't you dare say that," Char scolded. "There's a lot to handle around here these days."

"Every day. Kind of."

Char didn't hug her again. She stood quiet and still, listening.

"Either Grandma's upset over something or Liam's sad about losing Mom and Dad or money's tight—"

"And when is there time to worry about how you're feeling, J.J.?" Char whispered the words for the girl's hearing only. "Who comforts you?"

Fourteen was far too young to have to take so much on narrow shoulders, but J.J. gazed off toward the rolling green hills before bringing her attention back to Char. "God."

God? Char couldn't cover her surprise and J.J. frowned. "You're laughing at me."

"No." Char shook her head. "Not at all. I'm just trying to understand."

"It's not so hard." J.J. swiped her sleeve to her face again and shrugged. "When things happen, I turn to Him. When the bad stuff gets worse, I turn to Him. Because if He can't make me feel better, no one can. No one can fix all that's happened. Losing my parents, or Grandma being mad and grumpy, and Liam being so sad. I just keep praying to God to give us time. If we get enough time, it will get better. I know it," she finished softly. "It's getting to that part that's hard some days."

The faith of a child.

Char remembered that verse and how Christ called the children to him. How women followed him, with their children, clinging to His message of hope.

This bright young girl was doing the same thing. "We'll fix what we can," Char whispered as footsteps approached along the gravel. "Step by step. Day by day. Okay?"

J.J. nodded as the footsteps drew near. "I'm glad you're here, Char. Real glad." She ducked under the horse's neck so that no one would see her tears, and when Isaiah came through the wide opening, Char put on her brightest face to guard the girl's emotions.

"Ginger is holding her own." She moved his way and when he started for the horse and J.J., she caught his arm to divert his attention. The maneuver worked well. Too well.

He dropped his gaze to hers.

Those eyes. Warm and brown and deep and thoughtful. Caring. So caring. She could get lost in those eyes, in the strength she saw there. But conflict engulfed this family. Falling for this man would only add drama, and she'd opted away from drama purposely. And still it managed to find her when all she wanted was a simple life, caring for humble creatures. Animals didn't generally come with hidden agendas.

"Did you need me?" he asked.

"What I need is more coffee," she told him to steer him away. "See you in a little bit, J.J.," she called over her shoulder.

Obscured by the horse, the girl waved as Char moved toward the door, hoping Isaiah would follow. He did.

He followed her out the door, then paused about twenty paces up the path and glanced back. "J.J. doesn't want me to see her upset, so you're guiding me away while she gets a hold of herself."

"You know her well."

He dipped his chin. "She's a lot like me. We've seen it from the time she was little. We like fixing things. Making them better. We don't like stirring up a tempest. And we don't like feeling helpless."

"Those are pretty solid qualities in my book," Char told him. "When your life has been surrounded by tempests, it's nice to avoid them as needed. And with all that's going on, she doesn't want to add to the burden of current emotions."

He frowned, glanced toward the barn, then shoved his hands into his pockets and kept on walking, respecting J.J.'s wishes. "She shouldn't have to be looking out for adult feelings. She's a kid." He scrubbed his right hand to the back of his neck. "But she was born with a caretaker's heart and I remember doing the same thing as a kid, so I get it."

"She sees a lot, Isaiah."

His frown deepened. "You mean my mother."

"Yes. The anger. The unhappiness. And she worries about Liam."

He stopped again, staring into the distance before bringing his attention back to her. "I do, too, but some of that was my fault for letting Mom make decisions I should have been making. I thought it would help her get over the loss of Andrew and Katie if she had the little guy to focus on."

"It could have done that," Char agreed.

"But it didn't, at least not the way I hoped. Instead it put him in her crosshairs. I think Andrew's death reminded her too much of losing Alfie all those years ago. Of moving too quickly and spooking the horse. Making her bolt. She loves Liam," he continued. "She loves all of us, but she gets so entrenched that she can't see her way out. And now this, with Rising." He contemplated the house. "Will he make it, Char?"

She didn't enumerate the things that could go wrong. She grasped his hand in a gesture of reassurance. Once she had it, the last thing she wanted was to let it go. But she did. "I hope so. Let's set up a watch schedule. We all need sleep to clear our heads. If he makes it through the next forty-eight hours, we should be in the clear. Just in time for the rodeo on Saturday."

"The perfect celebration for horse-loving kids."

"Now we just have to heal the dog, stabilize the mare and not have a foal on Saturday afternoon. After I check on the other rescued horses."

"Well, Doctor." They'd reached the steps leading up to the back deck overlooking the ranch. They climbed them and Isaiah reached for the door handle. "I'm trusting this to your capabilities and God's hands. After seeing you perform on-the-spot surgery last night, I have absolute faith in both."

It was nice to hear, but when the horse rescue called to say one of the rescue horses had passed away overnight, and Rising spiked a late-morning fever, Char was pretty sure her veterinary practice couldn't have had a worse start in Shepherd's Crossing.

Chapter Eight

"I want Braden to come see the dog." Isaiah's mother folded her arms and impatiently tapped her toe against the broodmare-barn floor a short time later. "Braden knows us," she continued. "We know him. He should have been called first thing, and I made sure your father heard my opinion on this. He was wrong to take such a chance on an animal so beloved."

So, she'd berated his father already that morning. Or maybe last night, while John was still struggling with feelings of grief and culpability.

Isaiah sighed inside. His mother hadn't always been this callous. Guilt and anger had changed her. Why couldn't she see that truth and repentance could help?

"Young people don't always have the experience or wisdom to make good assessments, no matter where they went to school. You know that as well as I do."

He set the pitchfork to one side. "You're not implying that Char is incompetent, are you? Because that would be grossly unfair and inaccurate."

She scowled at him, hands clenched. "We have a seriously injured dog that meant everything to your brother, and now to his children. Maybe he'll do fine after being operated on in the dark of night in the back of a van, but what if he doesn't? How do we explain that to Liam?" she demanded. Accusation darkened her gaze and filled her voice. "We had the chance for another veterinarian to step in. A professional who is also an old and cherished friend. What if we lose that dog and we didn't take that opportunity to do the best we could?"

He didn't answer right away. Pausing gave him time to tamp down rising emotions. Did his mother hear herself? How critical she'd become?

"I know this girl is young and pretty but how can she know more than a man who's been treating animals for years?" Stella continued. "Liam's heart will break if anything happens to Rising. You know it. I know it. It's not a chance we can take, Isaiah. There is no need to bring more suffering when a family has endured so much. And a Fitzgerald, too, as if we haven't had enough of that influence in this town."

"Braden is welcome to give a second opinion." Isaiah splayed his hands. "I have no problem with that as long as he's polite. Dr. Fitzgerald—" he used her full name and title purposely "—isn't a girl. She's a skilled and educated woman and she has put her reputation on the line to help us. And her uncle bought that land fair and square. We all know that, even though people are angry that they lost an opportunity. How long should people hold a grudge, Mother? How long do we let old animosities burn our souls?"

It was a rhetorical question because he knew Stella wasn't about to answer. "In any case, the kids and I are grateful for Char's help and her expertise. She's absolutely amazing. You surprise me, Mother."

She'd dropped her eyes at the mention of Char's name. Now she brought them up quickly.

"To assume Char doesn't know her stuff is wrong and you've always favored empowering women to be the best they can be. And she is exactly that." He faced his mother and held her gaze. "If you could have seen her operating last night—it was remarkable. Her van is a mobile hospital. And Dad was a great assistant to her."

Being reminded that John assisted during the

surgery only deepened her scowl. "The daughter of a rich man with rich-man toys—yes, I know, but that's nothing to me when her family comes to this part of the country and buys up land, land, land! Land that had been in families for generations. And suddenly it's not our family land and pretty soon it's worth ten times what it was thirty years ago."

He wasn't about to rehash the arguments of inflation and money markets and speculation. She didn't care about that. She cared only that the Fitzgeralds, Carringtons and Hardaways bought land at a fair market price more than three decades ago and then invested thirty years of labor, love and money to increase their value. That, coupled with inflation and increased interest in buying ranchland, drove prices through the roof.

His mother didn't want to see the sense in it. "I'll call Braden," she insisted.

"Char and Dad will be at my place once we've finished morning chores. He can come any time after ten."

"I'll leave the timing to him. He is a busy man, a friend and your godfather. He deserves respect, at least as much as any newcomer, I believe. If you cannot respect me, you should at least respect him. A man who is highly regarded around here."

Of course he was highly regarded because he was the only available option. To have a new veterinarian, and a Fitzgerald to boot—that ruffled as many feathers as saving the falsely accused horse.

He left quietly, refusing to take the bait. Her arguments cycled, rarely wearing down.

Sometimes he tried to remember her like she was when he was young. Strong but kind. Forceful but caring. She'd been a leader among the women before the accident.

She was still a leader, but among a much smaller group. And they weren't the same people. Now she gravitated toward the discontented and fit right in with them.

Most of their family and friends lived peacefully, working their land or jobs. Living their lives.

How he wished she'd do the same.

"Doctor, you did what you could." The co-manager of the horse-rescue farm walked Char to her van a short while later. "It's hard on an old horse when the whole body gets tipped out of whack. At least he spent his last days being loved."

"I'm grateful you took the chance." Char shook the woman's hand. "But I'm sorry it ended this way."

"Us, too. But his buddy seems to be doing better each day. In a business like this, you go in knowing you can't save them all."

"I know." She made a face of regret toward the empty stall. "It's not like it was totally unexpected. But not the outcome I hoped for."

"Us, either. Still, if the others make it, that's pretty amazing considering the odds were stacked against us."

She was right, and Char appreciated her understanding and her optimism. She went back to Dancing Meadows to relieve John so he could do chores. He stood up as she walked in. He didn't say a word, but he took one look at her, handed her a fresh mug of strong, hot coffee and patted her shoulder. "The best vet I worked with was nearly forty years ago, when things were real different from what I saw last night."

He meant the amazing technology that let her drive around in a surgically-ready van to treat emergencies. "A lot has changed, that's for sure."

"One thing that hasn't is the dedication of the doctor involved, and he had that. So do you. And no matter what your last name is, Char, I'm real glad to have you in Shepherd's Crossing. I didn't see what we needed until it was right here, before me. Now I do."

Tears threatened.

She was tired and it was always harder to accept praise when she was tired, but she blinked the tears back and gripped the coffee. "Thank you for that. And this." She directed the mug toward the sleeping dog. "How's our boy doing?"

"Holding his own. We keep praying."

She might not be a believer, but she wasn't against the idea of prayer, either. Especially when so much was on the line. "It sure can't hurt, John."

He went through the back door. In the distance she saw Isaiah's truck parked along the far fence line. He moved from the truck to the fence and back. Fixing something? Or maybe just checking to make sure connections were tight. He didn't move fast, but he didn't lumber, either. He walked with solidity and focus, a man with the self-awareness to know he'd get it done.

He glanced up as his father approached. She couldn't see his smile from here, but she imagined it, then scolded herself for picturing it. She got that she was attracted to him. From the moment he showed up in Bitsy's pasture a few days ago, his presence called to her. Fortunately she was smart enough to resist the call.

She set her laptop on the table, powered it up and sat down with the coffee to check her emails. Liam would be home from school in an hour and J.J. was at camp. Other than Rising's breathing, the house was silent. As she went through her electronic mailbox, the peace and quiet of the Western farm surrounded her. The rustic beauty, the grazing horses, the sweet silence.

Head bent, she kept on working right until the doorbell rang.

She jumped.

When the bell pealed, the trusty dog tried to leap up. The meds made him groggy. He rose, stumbled and fell back down.

She rushed to his side, murmuring words of comfort.

The doorbell rang again, insistently.

Rising's head came up, longing to answer the summons. He barked piteously, an attempt to defend his home, his master, his territory.

She wouldn't leave his side. The door was unlocked. If the person had business with Isaiah, let them try the door. Or find him out back.

Nothing happened. No one entered.

Then the back door swung open. Braden Hirsch strode into the kitchen. He spotted her and wasted no time. "Isaiah wants a second opinion on the dog."

Her heart went tight.

She wasn't afraid of a second opinion. But the thought that Isaiah called this man in without mentioning it to her indicated he doubted her abilities. Or that she wasn't considered important enough to be informed. Either scenario stung.

"Clearly the animal is stressed." Braden crossed the room quickly. "He should be kept calm post-surgically, especially with internal damage."

She worked to keep her cool as she held the dog's head in her lap, soothing him with light, gentle strokes. "He was calm, thank you. The doorbell startled him. He tried to get up."

"What pain meds have you prescribed?" He asked the question in a quick, stern voice, as if she was a wayward child.

She wasn't, and she refused to let him set the tone. She kept her voice relaxed as she listed the meds she'd used.

"And you operated in your van?" Braden raised two bushy gray eyebrows in disapproval. "When there's an antiseptic option in Council at my practice? And several in McCall?"

"Are you familiar with mobile veterinary clinics, Doctor?"

He scowled. "Having stuff in the back of a van doesn't make it a safe option for invasive surgeries."

"Safer, actually, in many ways," she corrected him mildly, still stroking the dog. "No risk of cross contamination from sick animals caged nearby, and when time is of the essence, the mobile unit can respond as needed. I'd be happy to give you a tour of it sometime."

His frown deepened. He checked the dog's injured limb, asked several questions in a clipped voice, and by the time Isaiah walked in through the back door about four minutes later, Char was barely keeping a lid on her temper.

She shot Isaiah a cool look as he took in the scene he'd created, and if she wasn't cradling the injured animal, she might have kicked him in the shins.

For good measure.

"What do you think, Braden?" Isaiah posed the question as he scrubbed up at the kitchen sink. "Pretty remarkable, right?"

"I think it's a little late to ask that question since this dog was in need of emergency services last night."

Isaiah shot him a puzzled look as he reached for a towel. "Which he was immediately given thanks to Dr. Fitzgerald's availability. We didn't have to transport Rising and she had him in surgery within minutes of the accident. It was quite impressive."

Braden stood and faced Isaiah. "Motor-vehicle surgery isn't the same as an operating room for small animal care. Considering the amount of damage to this limb, an amputation may have been the wiser choice. Dogs manage quite well on three legs, and you limit the possibility of infection and further damage from shattered bone."

Up to this point Char had kept quiet from her spot on the floor.

She'd watched Braden's face, saw his open disapproval and heard the reproach in his voice while maintaining dignified silence. But to suggest that amputation was better than fixing a broken leg galled her and she couldn't stay quiet anymore.

She settled Rising's head back onto the soft rug he loved and stood. "Fixing will always beat removing, Doctor." She ignored Isaiah purposely. She'd deal with him later. For the moment Braden Hirsch was going to get a lesson in manners. She took a moment to wash her hands at the kitchen sink. When she was done, she turned. "It takes skill, practice and good eyesight to fix a GSW like that." She indicated Rising with a jut of her chin. "If the medical professional on-site goes into this kind of surgery with the necessary skills, then repair is the best option. If the professional lacks those skills, amputation offers a reliable alternative."

She turned and faced Isaiah. "I'm going to the barn to check on Ginger while you consult with Dr. Hirsch."

She didn't wait for an answer.

Head high, she went out the door, across the back deck and down the graveled drive, and when she got into the barn, she kicked a straw bale, nice and hard. And when that felt good, she kicked it again...

And then approached the recovering horse with a much better attitude than she'd had five minutes before.

"Infection, bone chips, debris, lameness. A gunshot wound is nothing to take lightly, Isaiah." Braden faced Isaiah in the broad kitchen and acted like he was dealing with an errant child. "A gunshot brings foreign objects into the wound. Something like this, with extensive trauma, is difficult to handle. The limb is bad enough, but to have chest-wall damage compounds the issues. We're fortunate the bullet missed vital organs."

"And equally fortunate to have Char close by," Isaiah replied bluntly. "There's no such thing as having too much skill when it comes to livestock and pets."

"That skill got her nowhere with the horse that died at the Council Horse Rescue this morning," Braden shot back. "Veterinary science has little tolerance for bleeding hearts. It takes the ability to make snap decisions and stick by them to be successful when dealing with animals and a rancher's bottom line. Like it or not, in the end a farm or ranch needs to make money. And it takes guts to make those decisions in a farmer's favor."

Isaiah clenched his hands. He hadn't heard about the horse. They were all hoping the rescued animals would make it once they'd passed the first few days. He was sorry to hear that wasn't the case.

"Part of animal triage is focusing the most good on the option most likely to succeed. Not trying to make the world a better place from the back seat of a fancy car."

Isaiah stared at him, shocked. "Did you compare a quarter-million-dollar operational facility to the back seat of a station wagon? Please say no." One look at the aging practitioner's face told him the answer. "Different doesn't equate bad, Braden." Isaiah waved his hand toward the segregated barn. "You're angry about the horse. My mother's angry about the horse, yet you both know it was the right thing to do. You can't admit it, and neither one of you wants to reckon with that old news.

"But we have to," he went on. "If this is ever going to be cleaned up and made right, we have to let the truth be known. These lies have been eating at my mother for all these years. It's time to stop. To come clean."

Braden stared at him.

For a moment Isaiah thought he'd made his point, but then Braden snapped his leather bag shut. "You're young, Isaiah. You think the truth will set people free, but sometimes that truth is what pushes folks over the edge. You might want to think about that."

Think about it?

He'd done nothing but think about it for decades. One bad day, one horrific accident and a lie of omission that had been on his mind ever since. Every time he saw Alfie's parents. Alfie's sisters. Or Braden Hirsch. No matter how much he tried, that old secret festered. Now it was time to cleanse the wound.

Braden walked out the door, climbed into his car and never looked back. And when he was out of the driveway, Isaiah checked on Rising.

The family protector had dozed off again. Calm, even breathing showed he was resting comfortably.

Char's coffee mug sat on the counter, still half full.

He brewed a fresh cup into a stoneware mug, the kind Katie had always liked to use. Then he crossed the graveled drive to the old barn.

He was about to enter the barn when a lyrical

voice drifted over the fenced meadow. Char's voice, light and musical, floating through the midsummer air.

She was singing an old song. A song about horses. A song he'd long since forgotten and now remembered because his mother had sung this same song to him and Andrew years ago. Before the accident. Before she'd grown bitter.

"When you wake you shall have all the pretty little horses..."

He came around the edge of the barn and paused, not wanting to disturb the scene.

She fit.

He felt it. He knew it. He understood the unlikelihood of it because his family had their own Shakespearean-style feud going with the Fitzgeralds and she was in the middle of discord.

None of that mattered as she walked the neglected horse gently through the field. And as Char's notes rose and fell, Ginger plodded along, nodding her head as if she liked the tune. Or knew the tune.

Impossible. Wasn't it?

Char looked up. Spotted him.

Her expression darkened.

He moved forward, ducked between the fence rails and took her coffee to her. "Fresh. Hot. Good."

She ignored him and kept walking the horse until Ginger put her head down to graze one of the few bright green sections of midsummer grass.

Not easily deterred, he followed right along. "I'm sorry Braden showed up while I was out back."

She shot him an incredulous look. "And I'm sorry you didn't bother to tell me you were calling a second opinion. It's your right, of course. But a professional heads-up would have been appreciated."

"I called in no one." He kept his tone mild. "My mother wanted a second opinion. I told her it wasn't necessary, but if she wanted one, it was fine. And I didn't see you to tell you because you were gone."

She held up her phone as a reminder of multiple options.

He acknowledged that with a grimace. "I should have texted. Or called. I had no idea Braden was going to hurry right over."

"So far I am less than impressed with the lack of hospitality I've seen in this community," she told him frankly. "I thought it would be different. Nicer. Lizzie and Melonie have both fallen in love with Shepherd's Crossing and the beautiful setting. They're ready to jump in and help make things better because they see potential in the town. In the people." She drew an unhappy breath. "I'm either hanging with a bad crowd or doing something wrong, because I don't think I've been scolded this often since junior high. And just so you know, Isaiah—" she faced him directly "—no one gets to do that. Ever. So your aging buddy should consider himself fortunate to be in one piece right now."

Braden had done a number on her.

Welcome to my world. But the moment he thought that, Isaiah realized something else.

He could change things up.

He had the power and the choices to make his world less divisive. Less antagonistic. "You're right." He frowned. Tirades had become too much of the family norm. That needed to change. "We've let sadness and anger take too much control."

His words calmed her expression. "Grief is an awful thing."

It was. He nodded.

"And these kids can't get away from it. Everywhere they look they must imagine what things would have been like if Mom and Dad were still here."

She'd nailed a big part of the problem because he and Andrew and Katie had partnered the Appaloosa ranch for nearly a decade. He stroked Ginger's neck as he answered, and the horse didn't shy away. She leaned in as if enjoying his attentions. "Every milestone comes with a shadow. Every holiday or birthday comes with regret, and I've wondered if that will ever get better?"

She sighed. She reached out and stroked her hand along the opposite side of the horse's neck in a slow caress. Her fingers, long, smooth and pale, contrasted with Ginger's chestnut tone. An opal ring flashed a hint of light as her hand soothed the old mare's months or years of neglect. "It does get better, even if it never gets fixed."

Was that the shadow he saw in her eyes? Wanting things to be fixed at last?

"For us, Corrie was the moving force," she told him as the horse continued to graze. "She never let us wallow in the should-have-beens or could-have-beens. With no mother and an absentee father, she was our everything. She took us to church, to horseback-riding lessons, to tournaments and dance recitals. We never really had time to think about what wasn't normal about our lives because she made it normal. She was there every single morning and every night. Even when she stood out in a crowd of wealthy parents, with her hand-sewn dresses and her fancy hats. Even when, every once in a while, a stupid kid would rag on me about having a black mama, the other parents showed her great respect. Like they knew she'd stepped into a void and made things all right again." Her hand hesitated, then stopped. "You know it never really occurred to me that she might have wanted something else or at least the chance to do something else."

The thought drew her eyebrows down. A tiny ridge formed and he wanted to reach out. Smooth the ridge away. Give her reasons to smile. To laugh. "She loves you."

"But what if loving us meant she never got a chance to live a life outside of us?" she asked. "She's traveled two thousand miles north and west, caring for family and friends long after the money ran out, when so many others would be opting for a Gulf Coast retirement. Not because she's supposed to. Because she wants to. So how blessed were we to have her in our lives and what would our lives have been like if she wasn't there? Or if she decided to leave?"

It was a rhetorical question.

Ginger plodded forward toward another section of tender grass. She glanced left and right as if looking for other horses, then busied herself in a new, shorter patch of grass.

"You're Corrie to these kids." Char let the horse go ahead. "You're their support, their person to lean on. The one who's there, 24/7. And how fortunate they are to have you, Isaiah."

She looked up.

He gazed down.

She'd been angry when he'd approached the paddock.

She wasn't angry now. She was caring. Lovely. Beautiful.

So beautiful.

Her ponytail swayed with every move she made. A few dozen freckles dotted lightly tanned cheeks. Not too many. Just enough. She held his gaze and when he glanced down at her mouth, her lips parted slightly.

Was she wondering, like him?

Wondering what it would be like to kiss him? Because the thought of kissing her had been on his mind from the moment she'd locked eyes with him in Bitsy's side pasture, and wasn't that an interesting turn of events, because he hadn't had the chance to kiss anyone in a long while. And now he wanted to.

He reached a hand to her cheek. Her jaw. And just left it there, to see.

She almost leaned into it.

But not quite.

She took a firm step back. "Don't mess with my head, cowboy."

He lifted one eyebrow.

"And don't do your strong, silent cowboy nonsense on me, either. I'm here to do a job and have already managed to tuck myself into a very Hatfield-and-McCoy-style land feud and your family scandal, and I've created a chasm between me and the old-guard veterinarian. I don't need casual flirting to muddy the already churning waters."

"No one mentioned the word *casual*."

She shot him a skeptical look as she came around to the front of the horse.

"And for the record, Char—" he paused just ahead of her, blocking her way "—I don't do anything casual. Ever." He let that sink in for about two seconds, then winked. "Just so you know."

Her eyes narrowed. She studied him before moving around him to unhitch the halter. "I'm going to let her graze on her own while I sit with Rising."

All business. Flat affect. Pretending she wasn't attracted. He might be rusty, but he wasn't blind, and he was 100 percent sure that Char Fitzgerald was just as interested in him. And even more annoyed by the prospect.

"Char?"

"What?" She turned impatiently as if to scold him.

He raised his hands. "Rodeo. Saturday. Evening show, as long as all is well here. Dad will stand guard over the animals for us. I'll pick you up at six, okay? That gives us time to grab food before the action starts."

"I can come with my sisters. They're bringing Zeke. It's fine—"

He reached out and tweaked her ponytail. Just a bit. Enough to get her attention, and when she raised her eyes to his, he smiled. "I promise that if you find me an absolute dud of a date, you can grab a ride home with your sisters," he told her, and he didn't drop his gaze or pretend like this wasn't very, very important. Because it was.

"Isaiah..."

"Make it five forty-five, actually. That gives us plenty of time to find four seats and grab food." He didn't wait for her to confirm or argue. He opened the gate, let her walk through it, then tipped his hat slightly. "I'll come back up in a couple of hours so you can sleep. And, Char?" He waited until she turned back. "I'm sorry about the horse in Council."

"You heard."

"Yes." He didn't say how or why. "And I'm glad you gave him a chance. He deserved that after what he'd been through. Just like her." He noted Ginger with a thrust of his head. "We do what we can, then it's in God's hands."

Doubt drew her brows together.

Doubt in God? Or in her choice to try to save the traumatized horse?

He understood doubt. It had plagued him for years until Andrew had pointed out the obvious. Something never comes from nothing. So how did everything come into being?

And then it made sense. Perfect sense in a most insensible manner, but from that moment on he'd believed. Seeing the unrest in her eyes, hearing it in her words—he wanted that quiet peace for her because Isaiah Woods was pretty sure Char Fitzgerald had never been able to claim serenity for herself, and if he did nothing else for this woman…he'd like to see that changed.

Chapter Nine

"So, the cowboy is picking you up?" Melonie exchanged looks with Lizzie on Saturday afternoon and grinned as she got things ready for Corrie. Corrie was watching the twins for the evening.

"And taking you to the rodeo with his two kids," noted Lizzie with that know-it-all tone in her voice.

"Who both have taken a shine to you," Melonie continued as she restocked the changing table with more diapers than any two eleven-month-old babies could possibly need in one short evening. Although Char knew precious little about babies of the human sort so she'd learn by watching Mel. From a discreet distance, she decided as she checked the charge on her phone. If the evening went downhill, she wanted to be able to call Lizzie as backup. "You two are ridiculous," she said as she examined her lipstick one last time. And then she gave her eye makeup a quick once-over again, too. Just in case. "We're working together, and the kids like me, so it made perfect sense."

"I have no trouble seeing the sensibility at all," Lizzie assured her, but she was grinning as she spoke. "You going out with a totally hot Western cowboy that just happened to wander into your life at the most unexpected time." She winked at Melonie purposely. "The two of us see that as quite sensible, actually."

"Because you happened to come north and find your one-true-loves," Char rolled her eyes as she exaggerated the words. "Doesn't mean I will. I'm doing fine on my own. As always."

Melonie laughed as five-year-old Zeke shot down the stairs, sporting his daddy's cowboy look in miniature. He slid to a stop in front of Lizzie, but only because she braced him with her hands so he wouldn't barrel into her. "Dad says I'm ready to go." He raised a hand and ticked off five cute little fingers. "I used the bathroom and brushed my teeth—all of them," he stressed to Lizzie because he wasn't a fan of sticking the toothbrush all the way into his mouth to reach the back teeth. "And I washed my hands and sang the silly song so they're like the most-clean hands ever!" He extended his little hands toward Lizzie and she made a show of examining them as the crunch of tires on gravel announced Isaiah's arrival. Char glanced at her watch—5:45. Right on time.

For a split second she wished she'd insisted on going with her sisters. Why was she doing this? Going to the rodeo with a charismatic single cowboy whose family seemed entrenched in drama?

"You'll have a wonderful time." Lizzie shoulder nudged her as Liam and J.J. scrambled out of the SUV. Isaiah followed at a more relaxed pace. "If nothing else this gets you away from work and out in public, where folks can see you're not the monster Braden Hirsch makes you out to be."

"Wow. Thanks."

Lizzie grinned. "You're welcome. And if your mind is on anything other than rodeo and cowboys with a date like that—" she aimed an approving look toward Isaiah "—then you've got more problems than a fun sisterly talk can solve, darlin'. I'm just sayin'."

"It's not a date."

Melonie coughed to cover her snort.

Lizzie pretended innocence. "Of course it isn't. It's just a pair of old friends who have known each other for a week, getting together to catch up on things."

"Char!" Liam spotted her through the door and raced in, then stopped, embarrassed. "Oops. Sorry. I should have knocked, huh?"

"That would have been nice." Isaiah was at the door.

J.J. was beside him, and with Liam framed in front, they were the image of a possibility she'd never expected and couldn't have.

Are you that stubborn that you refuse to open your eyes to new possibilities? So he's got a grumpy mother. And his godfather doesn't like you and thinks you're incompetent. Does that really matter?

Liam grabbed hold of her and embraced her with a hug that felt good. Really good. So maybe all the other stuff didn't matter like she thought. She'd been surrounded by discord all her life, and she came out all right.

J.J. came in and took her free hand. "I'm so glad you're coming with us!"

"For realsies?" Char asked and J.J. burst out laughing.

"Total realsies! I need your advice in the most sincere, professional way," she went on. "I saw a horse online. It's a grand jumper and I've got enough money saved to afford it, but Isaiah says he wants you to look at him before any decisions are made."

"You said that?" She faced Isaiah over Liam. "An experienced horseman like you wants my opinion?"

He shrugged. "I don't raise or breed jumpers. I know what I know." He held her gaze for a little too long, making her heart beat a little faster. A little stronger. "And what I don't know. But I'm not afraid to learn a lesson or two, Doctor." He smiled then, and that smile drew her closer. "If you come to see this horse with us, J.J. will know what to look for. How to examine a jumper for the best optimum outcome. Of course you'd be along for educational purposes only." He grinned when Lizzie made a doubtful noise.

Char ignored his flirting and addressed J.J. "You said he looks amazing? How do you know this?"

"They posted videos on the ranch site. He's broad and strong and a whole lot of horse, Char, but when he moves…" The girl took a deep breath. "It's like the wind."

Char knew exactly what she meant. "That smooth?"

"As if made for jumping. And made for me."

Char raised her eyes to Isaiah's.

He watched her with the kids. Then he

brought his eyes up and wasn't watching the kids. Just her.

She swallowed hard.

He noticed and that brought heat to her cheeks. "We'll compare notes tomorrow, J.J. I promise." He pointed to the country-motif clock on the wall. "Right now we need to go if we're going to grab food."

"I'm ready."

"Great." He opened the screen door, then held it open for the rest of them.

She let Liam hustle through, then J.J., and when her turn came, Isaiah was there. Right there. Holding the door and smiling at her.

Her heart fluttered.

In her world of stoicism, fluttering hearts were not allowed, but it seemed today, tonight, she had no choice. And when he opened the car door for her, then closed it with gentle care, her heart did that silly thing again.

And it didn't just feel wonderful...it felt right.

Liam took one look at down-in-the-dirt realities of calf-roping, burst into tears and cried inconsolably for a quarter hour once they had him off the bleachers and outside the arena ninety minutes later.

J.J. and Char wisely gave Isaiah some space with the boy. Isaiah sat on a sturdy bench and whispered words of comfort as Liam tried to gain control of his emotions, but one thing was clear. Liam couldn't handle the rigors of the rodeo and they wouldn't be going back onto the bleachers tonight.

Char approached once Liam had gained some control. "So, guys, how about giving the new girl in town a tour of the area?"

"There's not all that much to see," J.J. remarked, then clapped a hand over her mouth as she realized what Char was trying to do. "But it would be good for you to get to know places, right?" She hurried the words, trying to cover her tracks. "Since you'll be traveling all over to fix animals."

"My thoughts exactly." Char winked when J.J. sent her a rueful look.

Liam swallowed hard. When he turned his face toward Isaiah, it was like seeing Andrew's face, years ago. So much of his father in the boy, and yet he seemed to have gotten Isaiah's soft heart. "I don't want to ruin everything for everybody," he whispered. "We can go back in, Uncle Isaiah. I'm okay."

Trying to be brave. Trying to fit in. Isaiah knew that scenario too well to be fooled. "Well, I'm not big on having those little guys dragged through the dirt, either," he told Liam.

The boy's eyebrows shot up. "You're not?

Didn't you and Grandpa used to rope calves? When you were little?"

"Not much call when you've got gates and crushes to corral them," Isaiah explained. "But if you're on a huge spread of land, or running thousands of head of cattle grazing public lands, you might have to rope them to brand them. It makes it much harder to steal them if they're marked."

Liam focused in on that tidbit of information. "People steal cows?"

Isaiah made a face. "Some folks would rather steal things than work for them, so branding can be an important way to identify your herd. We graze on our own land, so we don't have a reason to do that at Dancing Meadows or at Grandpa's."

"Because our calves are all fenced in, with their mamas."

"And Grandpa wouldn't like it," added Isaiah. "He doesn't want the spirit of the animal wounded by the greed of man, so he doesn't brand. We never did." Isaiah set the boy onto the ground and stood, then grasped his hand. "Let's head out and show Char around while we've got Grandpa keeping an eye on things at our place, okay?" He lifted his gaze to Char. "Unless you'd rather stay with your sisters?"

"I would much prefer a personal tour, thank

you very much." She didn't take a moment to think about it, and her quick answer made J.J. smile. "I have to admit I wanted to dash across the arena and let those calves run free myself, so Liam and I are on the same page."

"Really?" Liam shifted his attention to Char. "You wanted to save them, too?"

"Every last one," Char admitted. "Blame my Eastern schooling or my Southern delicacy, but either way, you and I are in full agreement, my friend. Let's take a tour."

The rodeo crowd roared approval at something right then and Liam shrank against Isaiah's leg. "Okay."

The boy hurried into the back seat of the truck as if he couldn't get away fast enough. When they pulled away, Isaiah glanced Char's way. Was she disappointed? Relieved? Wishing she was anyplace else about now?

She met his gaze, sent a look of sympathy toward the boy in the back seat, then winked at Isaiah.

Kind. Caring. But strong, too, a strength he'd witnessed several times in just a few days. And he was pretty sure she was being totally honest when she said she wanted to save those calves from being roped and tied.

They drove north until they got to the turn-off for Shepherd's Crossing. "So, this is our little town," he explained, but there wasn't a whole lot to say about a half-empty town, was there? He drove slowly, still heading north. "It's fallen on some hard times."

"But doesn't the church look wonderful with its new coat of paint, Uncle Isaiah?" J.J. pointed out the bright white church nestled against a stand of evergreens. "Like a postcard. A whole group of people got together and painted it two weeks ago," she explained to Char. "We need a new pastor and the church needed some work. Who wants to be a pastor in a splotchy old church?"

"And someone is looking at buying these three storefronts on Main Street and using them for offices," added Isaiah. "That would bring some people into town."

"They asked my sister's advice," noted Char. "She had a meeting with whoever it is, and if you knew Melonie, you'd know that no sweet town is going to escape the makeover talents of one of Kentucky's finest interior designers. She got a cable deal to do a renovation show set up here, so she's totally psyched."

"TV? Seriously?" J.J. sat forward. "Our town is going to be on television?"

"They're going to start with the big Hardaway Ranch project that she and Jace will be working on all summer," Char told him, "but they've already lined up two early fall projects and they need ten episodes filmed and edited and ready to go by next June, so Jace is working on the renovation at Gilda Hardaway's house and Melonie is hunting up business."

Isaiah caught J.J.'s eyes in the rearview mirror. "Before you ask, J.J., no, we do not want to be renovated, nor do we have any desire to be on TV."

J.J. laughed. "Dad would have said the same thing. He wasn't big on people getting all up in one another's business. But I love seeing how things get done on some of those shows, Isaiah. And I'm pretty good with power tools."

"True. And I'm grateful for the help," he admitted. "There's always something getting broken on a ranch."

"Are we driving all the way up to the reservation to see people?" asked Liam.

Isaiah shook his head. "Too late in the day for that, kiddo. Another time, okay?"

"How far is it?" asked Char. "And how big is it?"

A question asked by many and still an understandable bone of contention among the Native Americans. "Big by white standards," he told her. "Confining by Nimiipuu standards. The reservation is 750,000 acres."

"Three-quarters of a million acres," she repeated softly. "That's huge, isn't it?" she asked.

"Uh-oh." Liam pretended fear.

"She's gone and done it now," whispered J.J., intentionally loud enough to be heard up front.

"Our tribal lands were once seventeen million acres." Isaiah waved a hand as he turned toward McCall.

"For how many people?" she wondered, and when he frowned, she put a hand on his arm. "I don't mean to insult you, Isaiah. But that's a lot of land left fallow if it never got settled."

"And that's the great divide," he told her as he pulled into a parking spot along East Lake Street. "Settlers pushed west, claiming what wasn't theirs because a new government told them they could. The Native culture didn't divide land—" he began, but Char interrupted him quickly.

"Sure it did," Char interrupted him quickly. "The tribes all had their areas, and some got along and some didn't, and the ones that didn't fought to defend their territories."

Isaiah parked the car and turned her way, but first checked the kids' reactions in the back seat. They'd been raised on this history, knowing and understanding the sacrifices that had gone before them. He couldn't let them be minimized. Not by Char or anyone else.

J.J.'s eyes had gone wide. Liam looked from one to the other, waiting for the implosion, an implosion that shouldn't happen because they'd come out for a nice evening together.

Char put her hand up to pause him. "I'm not negating the impact of the loss of tribal lands," she said gently. "Or the horror that followed in the Nez Percé War and how the people were sent into the Deep South afterward. The sorrows of war and the bad decisions of power-hungry people sicken me," she said frankly.

"I sense the word *but* coming," said Isaiah. "And for us, there is no *but*, Char. Lives were irrevocably changed not just then." He glanced into the back seat. "But forever. There were no options when Chief Joseph and the remaining people were captured. The tribe was gathered and herded south like animals, then kept prisoner there. Children perished. Old ones died on the trek with no one to bury them. Women wept and once-strong men felt helpless. It was a time of horrors, so the gift of a morsel of land that was already ours wasn't much of a gift," he said frankly. "And the reason our ancestors survived—" he motioned to J.J. and Liam when he stressed the pronoun "—was simple. We adopted the faith. We became Christians. It didn't make us one with the white neighbors back then, but it made us acceptable eventually. And in the end it spared our lives."

His words touched her. He saw it in her gaze, then heard it in her voice. "My maternal ancestors crossed the ocean in 1635," she replied. "They were repressed people who wanted the freedom to worship as they chose. The thought of this land must have been such a fear and an opportunity to begin again… My Irish side dealt with repeated invasions by Vikings, Normans and a host of others over centuries. Eventually the cultures merged, becoming stronger by taking the best of both worlds. And looking at those two—" she hooked a thumb toward the back seat "—I'd say you've already done that in so many ways. I'm not negating the sacrifices of history or the need to preserve heritage." She kept her voice soft, but she wasn't about to back down; he saw that clearly enough. "But assimilating into new circumstances is part of the adaptation that keeps us alive, isn't it? Life science 101. That which will not adapt will most likely perish."

"Science can simplify the definition of the process," he told her. "The human heart doesn't find it quite so easy."

"Yet that might be what strengthens us," she replied. "We bear up under the most difficult circumstances and adjust as needed. Our hearts and souls give us that advantage over all the other creatures. I think we're wise to use it." She reached for the door handle as she changed the subject. "I haven't been up to McCall yet. I've gotten as far as Young Eagle's place but never drove past it. What a nice town."

"Isaiah thinks it's too big," noted J.J. as she climbed out of the back seat. "But I love coming up here. Or going to Boise. Seeing the shops and the people."

"You like a splash of city mixed in. Me, too. But I love being in the country most of all," Char admitted. "Do you guys get to Boise often?"

J.J. shook her head, but then took Isaiah's hand in a gesture of unity. "No, but I can do that when I'm older. I do want to see things. Try things." She squeezed Isaiah's hand lightly. "But then I want to be home, too. Running horses and fixing things. And if I have a jumper to work with, that puts everything else on hold."

J.J. had a solid outlook on things, even without parents to guide her. Why did he feel the need to look backward so often? Why did he worry about offending some and protecting others? When it came to business, he was crisp and clear because he saw the bottom line and he not only expected respect…he gave it.

But he hadn't always stood his ground with

family and friends. Did the old guilt weigh that heavily? Did it affect so much?

It did and he was just now realizing it.

Liam scrambled out of the car. "I know where we're going, and, Char, you're going to love it so much!" He seized her hand and she went along with him, laughing. J.J. smiled, watching them, then hurried ahead to join them.

They formed a picture, the three of them, with Char in the middle. She was chattering about something, making both kids laugh and his heart loosened to see it. She engaged them. She engaged him. And she wasn't afraid to challenge him. He liked that. And when he noticed a younger cowboy quietly checking her out as she walked by, he had to fight the urge to cross the street and knock the guy over. Trouble was, he was doing exactly the same thing.

During the work days she wore loose-fitting jeans and T-shirts.

These jeans were not loose-fitting, and the white tank top reminded him of a favorite country song. When she paused, waiting for him to catch up, she turned and spotted him noticing.

She tipped her head. Frowned slightly, as if scolding him.

It didn't work.

He splayed his hands as if saying he had no choice, and couldn't hold back a smile.

She smiled back. A faint blush touched her cheeks, and he wanted to lay the palm of his hand against that cheek. Feel the warmth build.

Then she spotted the ice-cream sign. "My favorite summer destination! An ice-cream shop by the water."

"We can get ice cream and walk along the shore," he told her.

"Another reason to love it up here," added J.J. once they'd crossed the road to get in line at the popular ice-cream shop. "The lake. The hills. The forests."

"I know what I'm getting!" Liam pointed to the hanging sign listing the flavors. "Blue Bubble Gum, just for me!"

"Hey, good reading," Char told him. She squeezed his shoulder lightly. "And that Espresso Almond Fudge is calling my name. How could that combination ever be bad?"

"That's Isaiah's favorite, too." J.J. raised her brows. A tiny knowing smile tweaked her mouth. "Kind of funny that you both like the same things. Horses. Cattle. Dogs. And ice cream."

That's exactly what he needed, a fourteen-year-old matchmaker. "I'm pretty sure 75 percent of the people around here share all those interests," Isaiah replied. "Not so unusual in these parts, honey."

"And yet, nice, don't you think?" Char posed the question as the kids turned to put in their order. She gazed up at him, and he didn't have to think. He knew. And he took her hand for just a moment while he answered.

"Real nice, actually." He smiled down.

The blush deepened, and he'd like nothing better than to stroll the beach while munching a cone and holding her hand, but when Liam got his Blue Bubble Gum cone, he turned and grasped Isaiah's free hand. "Thank you, Uncle Isaiah. You always know the very best things to do."

So he didn't hold Char's hand.

But as they walked along the beach, watching all kinds of watercrafts buzzing the lake, it still felt good and right. Isaiah hadn't felt like that in way too many years. Watching Char shoulder-nudge J.J....

Laugh with her...

It felt downright wonderful.

Chapter Ten

"Isaiah, thank you." Char turned his way when they approached the stairs leading up to the stable apartment over two hours later. "It was a wonderful night."

"Not the night we'd planned." Regret deepened his voice but he relaxed when she laughed.

"Better," she assured him. "I realized that while I'm a great animal person, I'm not cut out for the rodeo. I was already worried with the first horse out of the gate, wondering how to fix the resulting injuries with my van twenty minutes away. Do you think J.J. was really disappointed?"

"I think any disappointment was negated by your agreement to go see that horse," he replied. "And there's no way I can say no when she's saved all her own money and has her heart set on something like this, so it's important to make sure it's the right horse. Who better than a steeplechase rider to make that assessment?"

"She's a great kid. And I love putting a horse through its paces."

"My brother would be so proud of her. Of both kids. Katie, too."

She wanted to linger. Talk to him. Get to know him better, but there were two kids waiting in the truck who needed to get home to bed. She reached for the door. "Let me know when you guys set up a meeting and I'll block time."

"Perfect."

She wished it was perfect, but would offering her advice just make matters worse at his place?

"It's important to J.J." He spoke mildly. "No one else's opinion matters, Char."

She knew better than to fall for that. "That's not really true in a family," she countered. "Especially a family that runs cooperative businesses and lives side by side. Believe me, I was raised in a house full of that kind of crazy and while I had Corrie to keep me grounded, it would have been so nice to avoid the drama of Grandpa always angry at my father and my father proving him exactly right once he had control of the business. All my life the one thing I've wished for is a nice, normal family. That's not too much to ask, is it?"

He pretended to think about it. "Define *normal*."

His answer made her smile and sigh because *normal* was a transient concept it seemed. "There's merit in that response. Thanks for a wonderful time, Isaiah." She grasped the screen door's handle. "I enjoyed myself so much."

He covered her hand with his. Glanced down at her mouth. Her lips. And when she was pretty sure that the incredibly handsome cowboy was about to kiss her, and equally certain that she wanted him to, Liam's voice broke in. "Uncle Isaiah! I gotta use the bathroom. Bad!" He dashed across the green space separating the matching stables and scrambled up the walk.

Char swung the door open. "Straight in, first door on the left, before you get to the connecting hallway."

"Thank you!" He streaked by them, effectively putting an end to romantic meanderings. That was probably for the best.

Isaiah directed a disappointed look from her to the boy's route. "Thwarted."

"Saved from grievous error," she corrected him as Liam reappeared. She pointed up the hall. "Go back and wash your hands," she ordered.

The boy stopped, surprised. "I did." He stared at his hands as if amazed she couldn't tell.

"Thoroughly if you want to work horses with

me. Twenty seconds, remember? With soap and scrubbing action."

"Like even at night? Like every time?" Liam stared at her, amazed.

"Every single time. It's standard practice when you work around animals, my friend."

"Okay." He trudged back to the bathroom, yawning.

He was tired. She got that. But if he really wanted to help, he needed to develop strong habits, and cleanliness was one of them. "Let me know if Ginger goes into labor overnight, okay?" She took a step inside as they waited for Liam. "I'll have my phone near my bed."

"I'll let you know."

"I'll come by to check on both patients in the morning."

"Thanks, Char." He laid his hand against her cheek for just a moment, and for that moment she allowed herself to lean into the hand and the strength of the man. "I'm grateful for all the time you're putting in."

She had plenty of time because her phone wasn't exactly ringing off the hook with local clients, but she didn't say that. Helping Isaiah and those kids was important. More important than polishing friendships with influential people by doing the wrong thing or caving to pressure. "I'm happy to do it." That was the absolute truth for multiple reasons. "And I'll admit that losing Ginger now would crush me because she's held on so well. Fought the good fight. I don't want this to end badly, so I'm available as needed. And then I'll use her for advertising purposes to build my business. If that's all right."

"Absolutely." His smile warmed her. Drew her in. It underscored his strength with a gentleness she'd never known in a man. She liked it. "A successful outcome is the best advertising of all."

Liam reappeared just then. "I counted to thirty real slow. Just in case."

Char palmed his head. "Good. Veterinary assistants can't take chances or be careless. Good night, my friend."

"Night, Char!" He hugged her, then tugged Isaiah's hand as he started down the walk. "See you tomorrow!"

She didn't return Isaiah's look of chagrin at their missed opportunity, but as the pair walked away, she touched her mouth, wondering. And when Isaiah turned at the end of the long walk, he raised a hand slightly. In the bright glow of the dusk-to-dawn stable lights, she knew he was wondering, too.

It was a question neither one should answer. But she went to bed thinking about the near kiss. The evening with him and the kids. The way he handled the boy's anxiety was beautiful. Clearly Liam's well-being ranked above the cost of missed tickets and Western fun.

Yes, she'd like to get to know him better. And sample that kiss.

But with so many reasons not to, why did she keep coming back to the foremost reason to do it…because every part of her wanted to see what it would be like to kiss Isaiah Woods.

And that was the best reason to avoid all opportunities.

Things were looking up, Char decided a week later.

Three spontaneous calls for veterinary services generated an uptick in her optimism. A sick dog, a cat needing to be spayed and a pig with a swollen and infected ear. Three people who hadn't blackballed her for either her name or for helping those horses against Braden's recommendation. Corrie's satisfied smile greeted her when she came into the kitchen to grab coffee and a homemade cinnamon roll the following Friday.

"It begins," Corrie noted as she frosted a layer cake for Heath's birthday. "People will call, they'll meet you and they'll talk. And then more people will call."

"Maybe not horse people, and there are a lot of them around here," Char noted. "But you're right. We have to begin somewhere and—" Her phone interrupted her words. She answered and grabbed the roll and her to-go coffee as she headed for the door. "Emergency," she called to Corrie. "Sheep attacked at a farm south of here. I'm going to see if Heath can assist." Heath knew sheep inside and out and he'd keep his head under pressure. That was an important thing in animal medicine.

Heath's number went straight to voice mail. He might be out of reach, or his phone may have wonked out. Cell phones had a way of doing that at the worst possible time up here.

She took a breath and called Isaiah's father. "John, it's Char. I've got an emergency call to Waggoner's Farm off Mill Creek, not far from you. Sheep attacked by wolves. I could use your help."

The older man didn't waste any time. "Meet you there."

If this was a human emergency, she'd be lights and siren and full speed ahead, but the curving nature of Route 95 slowed her pace. She turned east just before reaching the Council city limits, and spotted John's SUV heading down a road. She followed him, and when he rolled to a stop in a roughed-up driveway, she pulled up alongside him.

An old woman hurried her way. She wasted no time and jumped into the front seat of the van. "Go straight back along this path, punch left, then right past the old shed."

Char did as she was told. John followed behind, and when she eased the van past an old barn, an older shed and an antique-era outhouse, she came to a fenced-in area well behind the house, virtually invisible unless you were standing alongside it. "Head up alongside the fence about three hundred feet," the old woman instructed.

Char's fancy paint job on her van was going to hate her for following orders, but she did it. When she got to the spot, she pulled to a stop, arced a K-turn and backed the van through a broken opening in worn-out fencing.

Three sheep had met their ends.

Four others were critically injured, and beside them, a big white Maremma dog lay panting.

An old man knelt next to the sheep. Tear tracks marked his face and a shock of limp gray hair hung over his sweaty brow.

John came up alongside her.

"Triage first."

He squatted low beside her as she assessed the sheep. She shook her head on the first one, knowing it was too late, but the other three had a good chance if she could get things cleaned and mended quickly.

John opened the surgical side of the van as another vehicle crawled up the narrowed lane. A familiar vehicle. And when Isaiah jumped out of the truck and hurried forward, she'd never been so glad to see someone in her life. "Mae. Howard." He nodded to the old couple, then got down low. "Who's first?"

"This one."

John had retrieved the stretcher. The men maneuvered the ailing sheep into position in the surgical unit. John prepped that one while she did the same to the second sheep at ground level. And when Isaiah reappeared at her side, she handed him a syringe. Then she directed her gaze to the first ewe.

He didn't question.

He turned and with a gentle but deft hand put the sheep out of its misery.

Then he turned back, put the syringe in the biohazard bag and held the second sheep while she medicated her.

The wolves hadn't messed around. They'd gone straight for the throat on the first three, but either got interrupted or settled in for food because she was pretty certain that two of the injured ewes would make it. A couple of neighbors had come by to help. She had them move the lost animals out of the area, while she worked on the more critically injured ewe in the shade of the van.

Don't think about the wolves. Their choices. Or how this could have been avoided.

She focused on medicine, not on a predator's cruelty or owner's carelessness. She understood the balance of nature, and this tattered place with insecure fencing had "accident waiting to happen" written all over it. Two elderly owners, rotting fence posts and old sheep was like a tragic invitation to carnivores.

Isaiah and John stayed nearby as she worked: John to her left, Isaiah to the right. And as the heat built throughout the surgery, sweat began dripping down her face, into her eyes.

A cool, dry cloth touched her brow, then her cheeks.

Grateful, she looked up.

Isaiah's eyes met hers.

He believed in her. She read it in the quick exchange, the confident expression. He trusted her to do the job right and that meant a lot.

"Thank you."

A softer look brightened his eyes for a moment, then he got back to work, clipping hair on the big white dog, prepping him for treatment.

She heard his voice, deep and soft, as he

talked to someone on his phone long minutes later. Then he was back at her side. He blotted her forehead again, just as the old woman hurried forward with a collapsible tent. They set it up over the ailing dog, shading him from the hot summer sun.

The act of grace touched her heart, and when the old woman knelt by the dog's side, praying over him, Char almost joined her.

Isaiah's phone rang. He stepped aside to answer, then rejoined them a minute later. "We've got a couple of folks helping at the house and Harve is here from Pine Ridge to put the fences back in order."

Harve was a Peruvian shepherd hired by Sean Fitzgerald fifteen years before. He and his brother, Aldo, helped turn Sean's dream into reality. Harve's wife, son and infant daughter lived in a shepherd's cottage at Pine Ridge. Aldo lived in the second cottage next door to them.

"Harve Jr. is going to monitor the less injured ewes when we get them to the barn. But this one will need extra care. Let's take her to my place," he suggested. "She can give Ginger some company."

"You got room, Isaiah?" The old man peered up at Isaiah.

"In the old barn, yes. Dr. Fitzgerald comes

by daily to check on a horse and a dog. She can check on Freda, too."

"Freda?" Char asked, without shifting attention from the delicate job at hand.

Isaiah pointed out the small ear tag. Below the number was a hand-printed name in permanent marker—Freda.

She hadn't noticed that each tag had a personal name attached. The additional sweet gesture softened her heart. Sure, these folks probably should have sold their stock years ago, when they realized they were no longer up to the challenge of maintaining the herd, but calling it quits was hard on old farmers. She'd seen the same thing back east—farmers hanging on past their prime, sad that no one stood in line to take their place.

"Howard? Mae? I hear you had a bit of trouble up this way." A local deputy sheriff came into the small grazing area to her left. He looked around and folded his arms. "You know I was telling my Martha the other night that you folks might want a chance to retire from raising wool and lambs. It's a lot of work for little return when you've only got a dozen sheep, right?"

Char didn't dare glance over her shoulder at Howard because she could see Mae's face from where she worked, and the wan expression said too much.

"Hey, Dewey." Isaiah moved to the deputy's side. "We've got a crew coming to tighten up the barn and the fencing for Mae and Howard. I don't think any of us realized that things had gotten out of hand, so we'd like to help."

Char couldn't see the deputy's reaction, but regret deepened his voice. "Well, it might be out of my hands at this point, Isaiah. I'm sure folks mean well, but if a complaint comes in against an animal owner, then we've got to check things out."

"A complaint?" The old man's voice pitched up. "You don't have to tell me who's complaining, that's for certain. It's Braden Hirsch because I won't sell him my farm or support his brother in the election. He's been telling lots of folks that me and Mae are over the hill and even addled. Well, I might have a bad case of the old arther-itis in both knees and my hearing's not what it was but my cataract surgery cleared up my vision. Mae's, too. And with a little help on the fencing we're fine right here. Like always."

They weren't fine.

Char had realized that driving in.

And if neighbors jumped in to help them clean things up and reorganize, that was a lovely gesture, but what about after? When winter came and the two infirm adults tried to care for animals in winter squalls?

"We're not givin' up our farm, house or land, Dewey Martin, and you can tell that to Dr. Braden Hirsch for me." Mae's pale look had been replaced with twin spots of color in her cheeks. "He's been after this bit of land ever since his parents passed on nearly two decades back. It irks him that our piece stands between his two bigger parcels, but it isn't his place to force a pair of old-timers out of their home."

"Now, Mae, no one said anything about you leaving your house," the deputy told her. He kept his voice and demeanor quiet and easy. "But you might want to consider downsizing the animal side of things. Making things easier on yourselves," he finished in a kindly tone.

"First the animals. Then the old folks. Then the bulldozer. You can't say enough words to sweet talk us about Braden, Dewey." The old man's hands shook with tremors or fury. Char wasn't sure which. "He always thought this piece of land should be his. He was wrong then and he's dead wrong now."

"Did Braden ask you to step in, Dewey?" Isaiah posed the question straight out. "Did he lodge a complaint when he heard about the wolf attack?"

"You know I'm not free to say who did what, Isaiah."

"That's answer enough for me," the old man

sputtered. "Tell him Mae and I are doin' just fine and if he wants to see me in a court of law, I'll be there. But this property is ours and will stay ours until the undertaker says otherwise. You can tell Braden Hirsch I said so."

The old woman hurried to his side. "Now, now, Father, don't be getting yourself all wound up in knots over Braden. You know better. We both do. First things first, like always. All right, old fellow?"

She didn't use the term to challenge or tease…

It was clearly a sweet endearment and when Howard seized her hands in both of his, his face relaxed. "I hear you, Mae. I hear you. Right as always and I'm grateful for that. Doc, what about Shep?" He turned her way. "He's going to be all right, ain't he? He didn't look as tore up as the sheep."

He was right, the aged white dog wasn't as torn up, which meant he probably backed off the predators, and that created its own dilemma. A dog that couldn't protect the sheep didn't have much value in a sheep pen, but that was a discussion for a different day. "He'll be okay but he's going to be on limited work capacity for some time. That means he won't be limber enough to guard the sheep."

The deputy cleared his throat. "I can take him down to the barn for you once he's ready."

"We'll have Shep in the house, Dewey." Mae sounded firm. "He's not used to it, but if he's gotten too old to do the job then he's just right to keep us company over a long winter. Only the good Lord knows how many of those any of us have left."

"The house it is, Mae."

The men from Pine Ridge came up the path toward them. They had fencing tools in hand.

Her phone buzzed a text from Heath. Sorry, missed call, was up top, chasing a few rogue sheep. Sent Harve, Aldo and Harve Jr. to help. We'll handle stuff here for the morning.

Heath was a good man, a strong shepherd. What would he think about this mess over here? Was it salvageable, or should the old folks be closed down? She wasn't sure and a big decision like that required certainty.

The less-injured sheep had been moved to the barn below. John and Isaiah had put the critically injured sheep into the van for transport. They came back around while she snipped and cleaned the dog's wounds.

Howard watched from his spot. The morning's tragic events had unnerved him, but they'd have unnerved a younger man, too. He clasped his hands, then unclasped them as John ran the buzzers to clean another area of thick, blood-crusted fur. "He's never been an inside dog."

"But if he could use a rest, that's the best place for him," said Mae. "He might get a little bored if winter drags on. Same as us."

"Although last winter seemed hard on him. Kind of lonely like," added Howard.

"We can make all of these decisions over the next few days," counseled Isaiah. "Let's get the animals moved and things cleaned up." He turned to Char. "If you're not able to head down to Nampa to see that horse tomorrow, J.J. will understand."

"I promised and I'm not big on broken promises, but it isn't the best timing with so many animals needing care, is it?"

John spoke up as he worked to disinfect the surgical area. "I'll keep an eye on things at your place, like always."

"And you'll call if Ginger foals?"

"I didn't see signs this morning, but I'll call right away. Although you'll be hours away."

He meant that the foal would arrive before they got back, but how nice to have a skilled tech like John on hand. Char worked tiny stitches, eyes down, as she spoke. "You've watched over a lot of deliveries in your time, I expect."

John didn't deny it. "More than most obstetricians, I figure."

"And we'd need to leave first thing in the morning," noted Isaiah. They'd scheduled a ten o'clock visit to see the beautiful Dutch Warm-blood horse outside of Nampa. "I figured a 6:00 a.m. start, with time for a quick coffee on the way. To go, of course. And then we see."

"Liam can stay with me if he doesn't want the long drive," added John. "He might like hanging on the ranch better than driving more than four hours each way."

"You're probably right," agreed Isaiah. "Especially if he's on foal watch. He's pretty excited about finishing summer school today. Being on the ranch with you will probably sound better than a day-long road trip." He motioned Harve over to them while Howard and Mae followed Harve's son and the deputy to the barn. "Harve, can you guys get this fence up to par? I'm pretty sure the sheriff's going to have to shut Howard and Mae down if Dr. Hirsch has his way, but we might be able to keep them afloat for a while if we've got solid fencing in place. Dad and I are transporting the most injured ewe over to my barn."

Harve clapped his brother, Aldo, on the back. "Compared to stringing miles of fence at Pine Ridge, this is simple. We'll get it done today. Then we'll see."

"Thank you."

John and Isaiah transported the injured sheep to Dancing Meadows while Char treated the other ewes. She was almost done when Corrie and three local ladies arrived with sandwiches and sweet tea for everyone.

She glanced at her watch. Nearly five hours had gone by.

And when Corrie and Sally Ann, the kind-hearted cook from Carrington Acres, offered to help organize the small house, Mae welcomed the help, while Howard stomped off toward the small pasture.

So much had changed for the old couple in a matter of hours, a problem she'd seen through-out veterinary training. She'd witnessed kind-hearted folks with too many animals or people who didn't have the physical or financial means to care for livestock any longer.

She drove Isaiah's truck back to his place once she set the final suture. Helpful neighbors were assisting Harve and Aldo with the reno-vations needed to return the remaining sheep to their pen safely.

Isaiah had given her the keys to his truck. The adrenaline of an on-site emergency was fad-ing and she needed/wanted was a shower and a strong, hot cup of coffee, despite the summer heat. And who would have thought Idaho would be this hot during midsummer? Not her.

She pulled into Isaiah's driveway after a short drive.

Braden Hirsch's car was parked between the house and her van.

She didn't want to see him. She wasn't in the mood for a confrontation or a scolding after a difficult morning, but he was in the barn with her patients, so she had little choice. She parked the truck, climbed out, grabbed her medical bag and walked forward.

Chapter Eleven

Isaiah spotted her first. Concern deepened his gaze. "Braden, while I appreciate your opinion, Char's here now and she's got patients to check. Let's take this outside."

"Well, if she's going to green light unsafe conditions and ignore laws of human decency in the treatment of animals, I say she should be in on the conversation."

She didn't want to discuss this after saving multiple animals and having her own restive feelings about the Waggoners' abilities. "Treating animals and buying that old couple some time isn't exactly indecent, Doctor." She didn't pause to engage him. She walked by to check on Ginger.

"You have a heart for animals."

That was about the first decent thing the man had said to her.

"But this isn't about the grandiose act of saving starving horses. Horses whose owner ran out of money and time nearly a year ago."

"The sheriff found the owner?" asked John. "I hadn't heard that."

"Up in the hills, an old-timer who used to run horses and couldn't let go. Then he ran out of money. Got sick. He was put into a skilled-care facility. The horses were supposed to be sold by his son, but that never happened. So they starved until they broke free a few weeks back and wandered into Bitsy's side pasture."

Char wasn't ignorant to the similarities to what had happened to the sheep today, but the cases were dissimilar, too. "Howard and Mae have local friends. That was made obvious today in the outpouring of help that came right over."

"But friends aren't there 24/7 and that's the kind of care animals require."

"Those sheep were in good shape," she corrected him. "The remaining few were alert, well-fed and clean enough to pass a standards inspection. The fencing's being fixed. A good fence would have made all the difference last night."

"A useless dog and sheep without proper protection." He stared at her as if her words were preposterous. "I'm all for farmers' and ranchers' rights, but we have an obligation as professionals to make sure our patients are being treated right."

"You own land near them, correct?" She stopped trying to examine the horse and turned toward Braden. "How often have you stopped by to help? To be a good neighbor?"

"Don't pin this on me." He drew himself up. Braden was a tall man, but she refused to be intimidated by his size or his ego. "The fact that I own land nearby doesn't make this my fault. And it's unlikely they'd take help from me in any case."

From what the elderly couple had said earlier, she was pretty sure any offer of help from him would be seen as suspect. "Look." She moved close to him purposely. "I don't care what your little feuds are. Frankly I'm pretty surprised that folks up here dig in their heels the way they do. I thought this kind of pettiness was a more Southern tradition. Clearly I was mistaken."

He started to interrupt, but stopped when she raised a hand. "I don't care about your grudges and resentments. Or festering mistakes. I'm here to do a job in the present, not the past, so if you're asking me to sign off against the Waggoners so the sheriff can commandeer their remaining few head of livestock, the answer is no. I'll continue to assess things as the situation moves on. In the meantime I want to check my patients and I desperately need a cup of coffee. If you'd like to join me in that, you're more than welcome, Doctor. Otherwise I need to get back to work."

"Us, too." John started toward the door and motioned for Braden to follow. "I'll make the coffee, Char. Braden, you're welcome to join us."

The older vet stared at John. Then he gave John a look of disgust and strode out of the barn and to his car. He climbed in, engaged the ignition and spun the car around in a cloud of dry, gravelly dust, then drove off.

John didn't get upset by Braden's actions. He walked to the house quickly, as if his old friend's hissy fit meant nothing.

Char looked from him to the dust, then back to Isaiah. "That went well."

He shrugged as he made sure the injured sheep was resting comfortably in the thick bed of golden wheat straw. "You called him out justifiably. He'll get over it or he won't, but I think we're all tired of the tirades."

"Just so you know…" she said, without trying to hide the aggravation in her voice as he moved her way, "you guys up here have nothing on the Hatfields and McCoys."

The reference to the infamous feuding Southern families softened his jaw. He almost smiled. Then he reached out, stroked Ginger's neck and sighed instead. "I never thought of how an old wrong could dog so many days and weeks and years of the future. How it becomes that snowball racing downhill, just growing and growing."

"That either plows into something and explodes into frozen fractals, or sits, big and lumpy and imposing, until the seasons change and the snow melts. Either way," she told him softly as she soothed a hand along the old mare's neck. "The snowball disappears and life goes on."

He moved his hand at the same time she did.

His fingers touched hers. Just a graze. Finger to finger. Then palm to palm. And then he drew her hand up, away from the mare. Turned it over. He studied a scratch she'd gotten from the fencing earlier, then gently—so gently— he laid his mouth against the small wound and kissed it.

Her heart melted.

He brought his head up, but didn't release her hand. He didn't bring his gaze to hers.

He paused at her mouth, wondering…and when he laid his mouth on hers, neither one wondered any longer.

The kiss—*his kiss*—was like nothing she'd

ever known. And when he angled his head and gathered her into his arms to deepen the kiss, Char knew she was exactly where she wanted and needed to be forevermore.

Call her crazy.

She wasn't crazy.

She was at home in this man's arms. In his grasp, in his life. And when he paused the kiss, she might have whimpered softly…

Which made him smile and kiss her all over again. He broke the kiss when the slap of the back screen door announced someone coming their way. He dropped his forehead to hers and stood there, just like that, quiet and comforting for long, beautiful seconds. And then he said one single word. "Well."

She stepped back as footsteps dashed closer. Small, quick steps, which meant Liam was coming.

Isaiah didn't let her go. Not right away. As the footsteps hurried closer, he raised one thick, dark brow and smiled down at her. Then he released her, just before the boy skidded to a stop at the barn door. Liam raced in, oblivious to their emotions. The boy's bright-eyed excitement gave Char time to rein in her feelings.

"Grandpa said we have a sheep in here?" He spoke softly as he rushed to Freda's stall. "What's her name? Can we keep her?" he whispered, as if having a sheep was a lifelong dream. "We've never had a sheep before, Uncle Isaiah!"

"We can't keep her," Isaiah told him. "She's a patient and we had room for her. That way Char can take care of her while she's taking care of Ginger and Rising."

"Like an animal hospital, right?" Liam reached around and gripped Char's hand. "So, why don't you just stay here? With us? Then you can take care of all of them and I can be your helper!"

Isaiah hummed softly. Purposely. Then he slanted a smile her way.

But this wasn't a fairy tale.

This was real life. She hadn't come to Idaho with an agenda. She'd come for experience and to gain a reputation. She'd gotten experience, yes. But at the cost of her professional standing because she'd gone against the establishment. "I think we're doing okay so far." She squeezed his hand lightly. "I'll keep coming over and we can care for the animals together now that summer school is over."

"I'm so glad!" Liam spun as if finally unconstrained. "We can have all of August together and I promised my teacher that I would read something every day, like to a grown-up. And if you're over here, I can read to you, right?"

"I'd love it," she told him. "But now I've got

to check Rising. Isaiah said he was trying to lick the wounds, so we'll need to put a collar on him."

"He's got a collar from my dad." Liam frowned. "My dad got it for him special."

"A different collar," she explained as she moved to the van. "One that keeps him from reaching the sutures."

The boy didn't like the idea of more constraints on his beloved pet. He scowled while she put the collar on Rising, and when the dog banged the plastic shield into the coffee table a few minutes later, tears sparked the boy's eyes. "He can't see things now, Char. You blocked him!"

She sat down next to Liam and tried to take his hand but he shrugged her off. "I did block him, Liam. For his own good. It will take him a while to get used to it, but if he keeps reaching that wound, he could get a nasty infection and that's a lot worse than bumping into things for a week or so."

Liam wasn't buying it. He stood up, frustrated. "I don't want him stumbling and I don't want the stupid collar on my dog. He can't see!"

"He can see as he moves forward," she corrected him. "And he can see from side-to-side if he turns his head."

"It's to keep him safe, Liam." Isaiah kept his

voice mild. "It doesn't hurt him and gives him time to heal."

"I think you guys don't care about what it's like to be a hurt dog and bump into things and have people you love shoot you!" Liam stared at them, hands fisted. Tears streamed down his cheeks. "Maybe you should think about how Rising feels, huh? And not just your stupid ways to make him sadder than he is." He banged through the door and dashed off.

"I'll see to him." John had been on the back porch. He slapped a hand to the nape of his neck. Regret darkened his countenance. "He's mad about the accident and I don't blame him. If I could go back and fix it, I sure would." Chin down, Isaiah's father followed the boy out to the horse barns.

"Sorry." Isaiah looked from the recovering dog to Char. "I know the collar's necessary. Liam will work through it."

He'd have to because it was a necessary obstruction. "Kids don't understand the gravity of infections, especially after surgery. But—" Her phone rang just then. She took the call and hurried to the door. "Problem at Carrington Acres. Gotta go." She hurried to the van and drove fifteen minutes. Ty Carrington directed her to a barn on the right. Angus cattle grazed the upper sections of their ranch, black and red with a few spotted ones tucked in for good measure. But the inviting summer pastoral scene was diminished by what was going on in the foremost horse barn and when Ty gave her the lowdown, Char's heart sank.

Fever. Lost pregnancies. Runny noses and fever.

Ty Carrington had just laid out the basics of a deadly viral attack. The question now was did Char have the experience and guts to wage this war and win?

She hoped so.

Chapter Twelve

"I didn't want to be the one to break this to you." Braden Hirsch motioned to the papers in Isaiah's hand about ninety minutes after Char had left. "But someone had to do some research on this gal and I'm sorry it had to be me."

Braden didn't look sorry. He looked…smug. But then maybe he had a right to be smug because he'd dug up some really nasty information about Charlotte Fitzgerald, and he was correct about one thing: Idaho horse lovers wouldn't want a crooked horse dealer hanging around their barns or treating their animals. In a place where stealing horses used to get the death penalty, no one in Idaho took horse abuse lightly. Nor should they.

But this.

Isaiah stared at the printouts in his hand.

Char, involved in a horse-ring scandal back east.

Char, investigated for duping vulnerable people, making promises she never intended to keep and then shipping their horses to auctions, where they were bought by brokers for international slaughterhouses, all to gain money.

It couldn't be true, and yet he wasn't just hearing it from Braden. It was here, in his hand, printed sheets of news coverage from Central New York…articles documenting the procurement and sale of over thirty horses. And the name on the documentation was C. Fitzgerald.

Anger vied with embarrassment.

He'd sided with her. Given her access to the kids. Given her free license to be here, treating animals, when she'd callously taken those treasured pets and sent them to slaughter.

He couldn't believe it, but he couldn't not believe it, either, because the proof was in his hands.

"We've got tight horse circles here for a reason, Isaiah." Braden wasn't scolding him. He'd gentled his voice as if teaching a lesson. "Outsiders don't belong here and that's not because of us. It's because of them. Folks coming here, pretending to be one thing and really being another. If we let that kind of person take root here—" he motioned to the papers, meaning Char was "that kind of person" "—we risk too much. This isn't about her trying to save one horse for whatever reason, or trying to gain trust. It's about knowing that she's betrayed folks before. And she must have been pretty good at it to have scammed the owners of over thirty horses."

His heart wanted to stop.

It couldn't because there was too much to do.

He had kids to raise. Animals to care for. And a future here, a future he'd thought might include...

No.

He wouldn't go there. He'd been foolish as a younger man. He wasn't foolish now.

He clutched the papers in his hand as Braden said goodbye.

He wanted to throw them away. Burn them. Destroy the very thought of Char doing something like this.

He knew her father's actions had thrusted her and her sisters into deep debt. He knew that had to hurt.

But this hurt more. When a professional betrayed the people depending on him or her, how could they ever be trusted again? And the simple answer was: they couldn't be.

And that was that.

"Do you think we've got herpes, Char?" Ty asked.

Char wasted no time. A herpes outbreak could

devastate a farm, a town and a region if allowed to spread. "It could be, Ty. I'm putting you under quarantine. And we need to thoroughly clean this barn. How many pregnant horses do you have in here?"

"Just two more. We've been talking about breeding for sale but haven't moved ahead yet. Right now we're simply adding stock horses. You think it's herpes, don't you?"

"I think it's serious," she corrected him. "We'll let the lab confirm things, but we've got to move on worst-case scenario. I need to know who's been in here and where your horses have been."

"I can get the cleaning started." An older man moved forward. "I'm George, Doctor. I know the protocol and we've started moving the other horses into another area. Farther away. There's no sign of anything there."

"You'll need to keep a sharp eye out," she told him. "This spreads quickly and we've got to get a jump on it to protect them as much as possible."

"Well, we're too late for that," noted Ty grimly. "But if we can prevent further damage, that would be good."

She went through the necessary list of questions with him. Where had his horses been? Had new horses been brought on-site? Was there any recent trauma or stress episode? Herpes could hang latent in horses and re-erupt under stressful conditions. That was bad enough, but if it went into the neurological phase, the outcome became more grim.

"There haven't been any recent traumas or stress. I did take in two of the rescued horses, but they've been quarantined since they got here," he told her as George and a younger man began taking care of things. "Young Eagle was here looking at a horse last week, Braden Hirsch was here to revaccinate for rabies and I stopped by the horse rescue near Council to check with Ivy about some old-time saddles she was selling. I didn't go near the barn where the new rescues were being held, but one of them just died, right?"

She nodded as she checked the remaining horses. "Not from herpes, though. The cause of death was internal issues that stayed unresolved as a result of neglect and lack of food."

"Can we be sure?"

Was she willing to stake her reputation on it?

No. But as she checked the remaining five horses in this paddock, she found two with fevers and nasal discharge and one with urinary symptoms. "I had each horse tested. All results were negative for herpes."

"And yet here it is," he said softly.

It sure looked like it.

Char checked each horse, went over the rules of quarantine and made sure that the farmhands understood the importance of segregation and disinfectant. But even with all those measures, herpes was a formidable opponent in horse circles.

She left a long time later, after a series of phone calls alerting the state veterinarian at ISDA and local horse people who may have come into contact with Ty Carrington's horses.

And then she weighed the possibilities in her head.

Had one of the rescue horses been infected? Had the lab tests issued a false negative on one of them?

Ginger's symptoms were clearing up and she was still carrying a foal with a strong heartbeat, so she seemed clear.

But what about the gelding at the horse rescue?

Char went through disinfectant protocol, left biohazard suits at Carrington Acres, then drove to the Council rescue ranch.

Ivy came her way purposely. "You think Ty's got herpes there?"

"I think it's a strong possibility, Ivy." Char pointed toward the far pasture, where the remaining rescued horse lolled. "I know the tests were negative, but could the deceased horse have had herpes? Were there symptoms I missed?"

Ivy shook her head. "None. Lethargic, yes, but no runny nose or eyes or fever. I think he just had a tired heart and a worn spirit. I saw nothing to indicate illness. Just frailty."

That was a relief.

It might not be a definitive diagnosis by agricultural standards, but a true horse person understood the nature of the animal. "So where did Ty's barn get it?"

She shook her head. "I don't know. Ty and Eric are about as careful as it gets. Their horses are almost completely on-site unless someone rides into town. Latent infection, maybe?"

Char would love to assume that the horse had been pre-infected and the virus had reared its ugly head over stress of pregnancy or conditions, but there were no adverse conditions, and pregnancy wasn't considered a strain. She bit her lower lip, thinking. "I can't see it. Which means we may have something else going on. A carrier."

"Who's been there?" asked Ivy.

Braden Hirsch. He was one of the first names Ty mentioned, and the only one who'd visited the horse barn. "I've got to call Dr. Hirsch. He was there last week, giving rabies shots."

"Oh, man." Ivy didn't seem to be an over-the-top person. She worked hard to rehabilitate horses, but with a grain of common sense, knowing she couldn't save them all. "Asking him about infecting horses might not go over real well, Char."

Char knew she was right, but there was no choice in the matter. She put in the call from the van. Braden answered on the third ring. "Dr. Hirsch."

"This is Char Fitzgerald, Doctor. I need to talk to you."

"I anticipated this and I've got nothing to say," he replied in a terse tone. "Let the facts speak for themselves, young lady."

The facts? What was he talking about? She had no idea, but she had more important things to discuss and not much time to do it. "The Carrington horses you saw last week."

A slight pause ensued. "That's what you're calling about?"

"Yes. You inoculated them, correct?"

"I did."

"We've got a possible herpes outbreak in the broodmare barn. One lost fetus and three sick horses."

"Herpes? There?" His voice shot up, which was good. He might dislike her, but any equine vet understood the gravity of the quick-spreading virus. "Are you sure?"

"No, but the evidence points that way. I need to know what other barns you may have gone to after treating Ty's horses. If they were shedding virus, you might have been an unknowing carrier. I want to put those barns on alert."

More silence, and then he spoke up. "I went straight from there to Dancing Meadows. And then to Charlie Scoville's place, up near McCall. How did these horses get contaminated?"

"I don't know that, yet," she told him. "I'll contact Isaiah and his father and then go up to Scoville's."

"Have you notified the state?"

"First thing I did. We need full cooperation to keep this from spreading. I'll keep you updated. If you think of any other place you might have gone, let me know." She disconnected the call and started the engine. She was a little worried about the reception she'd get from the Woods family. She'd hurt Liam earlier by collaring his trusted friend. Given the choice, she might have kept her distance for a little while to give him time to calm down, but this news wasn't a simple inconvenience.

This was a game changer for horse breeders. She put the van into gear and headed back toward Isaiah's ranch, feeling heartsick and wishing she had better news.

Isaiah was crossing the drive, moving toward his truck. He paused when he saw her.

There was no welcoming smile on his face. No warmth in those dark brown eyes. He stared at her as if...

As if she were the enemy.

She climbed out of the van and moved his way. He halted her by raising one hand up, and in that hand he clutched a folded paper. "You've got a heart for horses, right?"

His tone was harsh and hard. She hesitated before answering, but then she didn't answer because she wasn't about to deal with anyone's bad attitude ever again. "What's this about?"

He unfolded the paper. There were several sheets, she realized then. And each one was a separate blog article about her involvement with the horse-selling scandal in Central New York. "Veterinary Student Cons Gullible Horse Owners." He read the headline out loud, then went straight to the next one. "Cornell Veterinary Senior Ringleader in New York Horse Scam. There are three more here, Char. Would you like me to read them?"

Her heart.

It fairly stopped right there in her chest because she'd proven all that wrong last winter. She'd stood her ground, put her chin in the air and finished at the top of her class even as scandal raged around her on personal and professional levels.

She'd survived because she wasn't about to let another person's vice and avarice bring her down. Not her father's, not her old boyfriend's... no one's.

But this.

That Isaiah would buy into this and accuse her, no questions asked, hit deep after he'd witnessed her work with neglected horses.

Her chest went tight but she shoved down those emotions, even if it took all the courage she could muster. "I'm not here to discuss old news."

"Of course you're not, because no self-respecting horse person would let you near their horses," he shot back. "I know your father did you wrong—I've seen the news reports—but conning people out of their horses by promising them a forever home and then selling them to slaughterhouse buyers isn't the way we do things out here." He waved the papers as if they proved her wrongdoing. "Is that how you paid for the fancy van? For veterinary school? Because most folks just take out loans."

He thought that little of her.

Four hours ago she'd kissed him. And he'd kissed her. She'd let her foolish head get filled with those silly fairy-tale dreams she never should have let herself entertain because she knew better.

And now this. Proof that she was right, that little-girl dreams of normalcy and happy-ever-afters didn't exist. "Believe what you want." She kept her voice flat to match his. "I came here because it's possible that the Carringtons have a herpes outbreak. Braden Hirsch was there last week. He was giving shots and came here when he left. If the horses were in the early stages and shedding virus, it's possible he brought it to your barn."

The word *herpes* shifted his attention instantly. "Are you sure?"

"The indications are there. The state's been notified. They'll confirm the lab testing."

His face clouded. He glanced back toward the broodmare barn. "What if I sent off infected horses in that deal last week?"

The thought of spreading herpes would bother any good horseman. The dreaded virus could cause grave illness and death. But reassuring him was about the last thing on her mind right now.

He'd been given half a story by someone. Braden, most likely. That explained the veterinarian's odd initial response to her phone call.

But that wasn't the troubling thing.

He bought into it without asking her.

She was familiar with the articles he had in hand, printouts from online bloggers. If he'd checked further, he'd have seen her name cleared of any wrongdoing by New York investigators. But he didn't check further. And that hurt most of all.

She climbed into her van. Right now the beauty and cost of the mobile clinic mocked her. She wanted to cry, but there wasn't time for that. She put the van into gear, did a U-turn and drove away, the sweet hopes and dreams of the morning gone.

Her throat hurt.

Her head ached.

But there were horses, magnificent animals, facing a life-threatening disease and that took precedence. She raised her chin, hit the gas and headed north on Route 95, toward the Scoville farm, southwest of McCall. She wouldn't think about Isaiah or those kids or the ranch they'd worked so hard to build, now threatened.

He'd go his way.

She'd go hers.

And if there was any way to make this required year of staying in Western Idaho go faster, well…she'd do it. Because a year of being scorned didn't make the short list.

* * *

Herpes.

Isaiah raced to the broodmare barn. The horses had been turned out that morning, before the intervention at Waggoners' farm. They'd looked fine from a distance…

And seemed fine now, as he drew closer.

But he wasn't about to be fooled, because he understood the danger. He called his parents right away and explained the situation. They came to the area quickly. Liam had been at his grandparents' house. Isaiah pointed toward the yard. "Liam, this is a contagious disease, so I need you to stay away from the barns and the fields for a while, okay?"

"But I know how to wash up now." He stared at Isaiah from the graveled drive's edge. "Char showed me and I do it all the time."

"This is different," Isaiah told him. "If we have this infection, it kills horses, Liam. I need you to listen to me. Got it?"

Liam fisted his hands. He stared up at Isaiah, then his grandfather. When John slung his arm around the boy and nodded, Liam stepped back. "First you show me what to do so I can help with horses, then you won't let me, and I bet that's 'cause Char isn't here. She likes me. She teaches me stuff that I want to know because she thinks I'm smart."

"You need to listen to Isaiah and your grandfather," snapped his grandmother. "When they speak, you need to listen. That is what a child does."

Wide-eyed, Liam gazed up at Isaiah. He swallowed hard, clearly hoping Isaiah would step in, but he couldn't. In this case Liam needed to listen and obey. A little boy, potentially tracking a virus from place to place, couldn't be allowed to run loose. "Rising needs you, Liam. And I can't spend the right time with him if we're fighting a virus out here. I don't want him to feel abandoned."

The boy's angst cleared somewhat. "Me and Char will take care of him and Ginger and the sheep," he declared. He started for the house with more confidence.

Should he tell the boy that Char wouldn't be back?

Not now. He had enough to handle at the moment.

But when his mother shot him a sharp, smug look, he realized that Braden had shared Char's past with her.

The two of them dwelled in negativity.

He didn't have time to consider the sadness of that while facing the possibility of losing these mares and their foals to a disease that could cause grave neurological malfunctions. A disease with no treatment and no cure.

He and his father did temperature checks. No fever.

That was good, but Isaiah knew that horses could go days or weeks with no symptoms. And then...

Havoc.

He made it through days one and two, and by the morning of day three, when none of the animals showed elevated temperatures, he entertained hopes that they'd escaped infection.

That afternoon, two of the broodmares spiked a fever. His heart sank.

They'd separated the newly pregnant mares to the far upper pasture, and they'd made a similar move for the stallions and young geldings and fillies.

But here, in the barn filled with life-giving potential, five pregnant mares were beginning to show signs of the dreaded disease and there wasn't anything Isaiah, his father or Braden could do about it.

Chapter Thirteen

Lizzie and Heath came searching for Char once they tucked Zeke into bed. Char heard Lizzie call her name.

She didn't want to acknowledge the call. The last thing she wanted to do was talk about the past or the present right now, but the equine emergency left her no options. Jace and Melonie joined them in the big living room of the ranch house, and worry deepened every expression. A deadly viral breakout had that effect on horse owners universally.

Heath and Jace took seats on the chairs facing the extended sofa and love seat. Lizzie, Melonie and Corrie sat closer to Char. Lizzie wasn't one to beat around the bush. She hunched forward, hands on her knees. "So, what do we do to prevent this virus from spreading?"

Char ticked off her fingers with rules they all

knew already. Well, all but Mel, who purposely gave horses some extra space. "We don't allow any horses on the property. Same for your two," she instructed Jace and Melonie. "Don't let anyone ride in at your place. No exceptions. No one from another farm is allowed near the horse barns or grazing. We self-quarantine and use biohazard protocol to make sure no one tracks the virus in. Foot coverings, gloves, full biohazard disposable suit if we can afford them."

"Already ordered—due in tomorrow," Heath told her. "We can't afford not to be the most careful. And don't be insulted if I ask you to stay clear of the horse barns unless absolutely needed."

"That's not an insult," Char assured him. "That's just plain smart. And I'd suggest we trade sleeping arrangements until we're clear. I'll move into the house and you and Lizzie sleep in the upstairs apartment. That keeps me clear of the barns altogether."

"We can pretend it's the honeymoon we delayed until winter," joked Heath, but he nodded. "Anything that keeps the virus at a distance is good self-protection. What are the chances you might have already brought the virus here, Char?"

She hated that thought, but she answered him honestly. "Slim, but possible. Viruses have a short life span in the air but if they get trapped in dirty boots or moist areas, they're more likely to thrive."

"You think it was the neglected horses, Char?" asked Jace. "They were in pretty bad shape."

"They've all tested negative and Ty segregated the two at his place, so it's never gotten within thousands of feet of his other horses."

"What about the rodeo? Horse gatherings are common disease-sharing sites," said Melonie.

"Except none of these horses were near the rodeo and Ty didn't go over at all. And there were no reports of sick horses brought in."

"So, where did the virus come from, Char?" Heath looped an arm around Lizzie in a sweet, natural gesture of protection and love. His action reminded Char of those precious moments in Isaiah's arms. His embrace. It took effort to shove those emotions aside.

"The state will update us as more cases come in. Maybe we'll be fortunate and this was an isolated incident," she told them. "They usually find the source unless it's a spontaneous event, a latent case that roars back to life. It's possible that it only hit Ty's barn."

"And he'll be meticulous about handling it," Jace said. "He always is."

"You alerted the other possible places?"

asked Corrie. "Is that why you were so late coming back?"

It was part of the reason, so she nodded. "First, Dancing Meadows. Then I went up north to warn the Scoville family and go over self-quarantine regimens with them."

"How did Isaiah handle this?" asked Heath. "He's just gotten those mares to the point of delivery and it's been a long road for their family. This has to make him nervous."

She hesitated a moment too long and Lizzie pounced. "What's going on, Char? What's happened?"

She took a breath…

A deep one…

And told them what happened with Isaiah.

"He really thinks you were part of that whole deal?" Heath jumped to his feet instantly. So did Jace, and Char was pretty sure her two new brothers-in-law were willing to leap to her defense. "You were cleared completely. Anyone with a brain would know you wouldn't have your veterinary license if you were found guilty of something like that."

"He seemed willing to believe what others were telling him without looking for answers for himself—or asking me. Which says a lot about him and less about me," Char told them. She didn't say that he'd broken her heart, but when Lizzie exchanged a look with Mel, Char was pretty sure they'd figured that part out.

Her fault, of course. Who fell in love with someone they'd just met? Who saw someone and instantly read the word *destiny* written in the clouds?

No one. At least no one with common sense, so that made this debacle as much her fault as anyone's. She wasn't here to find everlasting love.

She was here to help establish the ranch and exercise her skills while doing so. That made it her problem for getting schoolgirl silly. "He'll have Braden to take care of things over there. Hopefully they won't be affected. In the meantime Ty gave me permission to experiment with a new treatment."

Those words got everyone's attention. Lizzie sat forward quickly. "What treatment?"

Char explained some recent findings and Jace whistled softly. "Giving them heparin might help prevent losing the mare? How did you hear this?"

She jabbed a finger toward the laptop. "I get updates from Penn Veterinary and American Veterinarian. It's big news in horse circles, but it's not a cure-all. It interrupts the progress of the disease although foal loss is still problematic. In spite of that, there have been impressive results while the horse fights off the virus."

Heath and Lizzie set up a schedule to check equine temperatures until the scare was over.

When Jace and Melonie had gone home, and Heath and Lizzie had gone to the horse-stable apartment, Char walked onto the porch. And then she sighed.

Maybe she wasn't supposed to be here. Or maybe the mobile unit was a foolish experiment, doomed to fail.

She'd stepped from one drama-filled problem into another, and while a few of the locals liked her, the majority might see her as a lying schemer once word got out. Maybe they'd believe the DA's report that she was totally innocent, but then didn't that make her seem stupid? For trusting the wrong man?

"My sweet girl wears the weight of an angry world on her shoulders right about now." Corrie spoke softly from the screen door. She opened it quietly and stepped through. "And that is way too much for one who's done no wrong." Corrie wrapped her arms around Char in a hug that Char didn't know she needed until that moment. "Folks here will see your true colors shine, just like they did in New York. A person who deliberately smears another's good name is a sorry soul in need of prayer, because the truth will come out. It always does. And you are strong enough to weather any storm."

"The truth will set us free." She leaned into the curve of Corrie's shoulder. "You've taught me that from the beginning."

"From the gospels, yes." Corrie settled her head against Char's in a gesture of motherly comfort. "Where does my strength come from? My strength comes from the Lord, who made heaven and this very earth we walk on," she paraphrased. "So I pray for my girls. I pray for the men they love and who love them. I pray for these children, little Zeke, these baby twins. And for Isaiah's children, their parents gone too soon, surrounded now by angry voices. For how does a child grow brave and true when so much negativity surrounds them?"

"They have Isaiah." Was it normal to instantly leap to his defense? Or unspeakably needy?

"A good man of strength and kindness, although my opinion of him is not the same this evening." She squeezed Char's shoulders in a telling gesture. "No one gets to assume bad things about my girls. Not now. Not ever. And I will have no problem letting him and his whole family know that."

"Corrie—"

"Hush, child." Corrie's voice meant business and no one dissed Corrie. Ever. "We Fitzger-

ald women have been sticking up for one another from the get-go. It's not about to stop now
and sometimes a good old-fashioned purse-
whompin' is what's needed. Verbally speak-
ing, of course."

"How about we let time work wonders," Char
suggested. "Another lesson you taught me."

"Well, there's that." Corrie huffed a little.
"You focus on getting those horses well. We'll
carry the rest."

The courier arrived with the heparin early
the next morning. When two other Carrington
horses spiked a fever, they were brought to the
quarantine barn, where Char administered the
first of their twice-a-day injections.

And then they waited, hoping to prevent the
neurological symptoms that took far too many
horses to the grave.

"We've got two horses with elevated temps,
Isaiah."

Isaiah had been cleaning out the shaded area
they'd erected seven years back, a broad open
structure to ease the heat of summer sun. It
was a favorite equine gathering spot for horses
in this particular pasture, but they'd moved all
the horses upland. It was harder for the virus to
move up than drain down. His father's words

sounded hollow, and John Woods only sounded hollow over tragic events.

Call Char.

He chased the thought away. Why would he do that? Why would he even think that?

But as he withdrew his phone to call Braden, the niggling thought came again.

He brushed it aside.

"I've already called Braden. He's on his way but you know the score," John said softly. "We both do."

So close.

They'd been so close to having new foals for future sales. New life, new blood. New lines of their cherished Appaloosas, more like the original horse that drew Nimiipuu fame two centuries before, when white men first traveled the path from east to west.

"No spread as yet." He motioned to the upper pastures as they strode to the lower barn. "That's the upside. For now."

Call Char.

The niggling voice came again, nudging him.

He couldn't.

She made the right call about Ginger. About those other horses. What harm is there in calling her? Are you that prideful that you can't open the door to peace between you?

That was just it. He didn't want peace between them. He wanted a future for them, and that couldn't happen. He'd lived with enough deceit in his life. Saving Ginger was his way out of that abyss. How could he rationalize her deception? Her choice to cheat people for financial gain?

He couldn't. He understood money problems. Strong finances were never a given in ranching. A bad year strained you. Two bad years could break you.

But he would not be broken. One way or another they'd go on, because Dancing Meadows wasn't just his legacy…

He heard J.J. call Liam's name from the old barn as she tended Ginger.

It was theirs.

Liam had been watching them from the bend in the drive. He'd followed their direction about staying away from the horses, and he'd busied himself with Rising and the recovering ewe, but Isaiah read the hunger in the boy's gaze as he watched from afar. So much like his father. Wanting to make things better.

"Liam, can you help me with Ginger?" J.J. called.

Liam turned, excited. "Sure! Maybe Char will come today and see how good Ginger's doing!" He raced to the old barn, excited by the invitation to help.

"J.J. has really stepped up to the plate to help," noted John as they moved into the paddock adjacent to the quarantine barn. "She's got a head for horses. And ranching. You decide about that warmblood yet?"

"No," Isaiah answered, too quickly. He sounded sharp because he felt sharp. And hollow. Then sharp again. "We can't bring him here under these circumstances, so we're holding off. If he's still there next month, we'll see. If he's sold, we'll look elsewhere."

"J.J. said she wanted Char's opinion, either way."

Isaiah didn't want to discuss this, but when his father went on, it seemed he had little choice in the matter.

"That young woman is a horseman's vet," John went on as he worked to disinfect the areas they'd blocked off. "She sees beyond the body and into the soul of the animal."

"While conning people out of their horses?" It made no sense. He shrugged one shoulder and got to work. Disinfecting gave them something to do while waiting for Braden to arrive and tell them there was nothing they could do but wait.

Isaiah hated waiting.

"You know," John went on in an easy tone, as if they weren't on the brink of disaster. "You get a lot of your qualities from me. Generally you look to the heart of the matter, you don't overreact and you grew up a fair man, always looking at both sides of an issue. Why do you think you messed up when it came to that young veterinarian and the stuff you read?"

That was a no-brainer. "Because a good person doesn't swindle vulnerable people out of their horses and then expect to be trusted saving horses' lives."

"And a fair person investigates the truth of the matter," his father continued. "Maybe finds out things aren't exactly what they seem."

He'd read the articles from start to finish. Every last implicating word. But his father's tone and the look he gave him indicated something else.

"I get that she saved Rising," Isaiah said. "And she's great with the kids and she stepped up to the plate for those neglected horses, but that doesn't erase the past, does it?" He paused the disinfectant hose and faced his father. "You're a horseman, Dad. You raised us to love and respect the heart of the animal. To unleash their highest potential. And helped to develop an Appaloosa worthy of our ancestors. So either talk straight or let's work in silence."

John stayed quiet.

He did that on purpose, Isaiah knew. To make Isaiah think for himself. Draw his own conclusions. And that always meant that his current conclusions were wrong.

When he finally got back to the house, he stared at his laptop. He wanted a shower and sleep, but his father's words pulled him forward. And when he Googled Char's name and the horse scandal, the truth didn't blindside him. It gut-punched him. She'd been used by a stinkin' liar. A man who used her name and identification to pull off lousy deals and bilk money from gullible horse owners.

And Isaiah had waved those foolish printouts at her like he was a judge and jury.

He'd let himself be foolishly used by Braden. And when his father woke him to say they'd lost two foals in utero, it seemed like the clock wasn't just ticking. It was ticking down to the eventual explosion.

Chapter Fourteen

Char got a call from J.J.'s phone the next afternoon, but when she answered the call, it was Liam's voice that greeted her. "Char, it's me!"

"Liam." Oh, that sweet boy. It did her heart good to hear him, to talk to him. She knew he'd come to count on her presence. Someone to talk to, to work with. "How are you, buddy?" She was in the middle of measuring meds so she put him on speakerphone. She didn't ask if his uncle knew he was calling. She could figure that answer out on her own. But since he did call, she wasn't about to shrug him off.

"I miss you," Liam went on. "J.J. lets me help with Ginger and the sheep but I miss you because you tell me stuff. But I'm not calling about me or you or anything like that. It's the horses, Char. They're sick. Like really sick. Uncle Isaiah is scared and Grandpa is scared and Dr. Hirsch is scared, too. And all I could think of was to call you and have you come and fix things."

The virus had spread.

Her heart sank to hear it, and the boy's entreaty touched her. How she wished it was that easy. It wasn't. "You've got a doctor there, sweetie. Dr. Hirsch has been taking care of your horses for a long time. He'll do all right."

The boy stayed silent so long that she tapped the phone to make sure she hadn't lost the connection. And then he spoke. "They won't be okay. I can tell because Uncle Isaiah looks so sad."

Char had prepared for a possible larger-scale outbreak by ordering more heparin. Did she dare just show up at Isaiah's ranch? Treat his horses? Risk the anger and accusations?

Corrie came across the room with a look of intent. It was an expression Char knew well, which meant she should listen. "Liam, hang on a minute, will you? I'll be right back."

"Okay."

She muted the phone and Corrie wasted no time. "When the good Lord was faced with adversity, He met it head-on. When they shoved that wicked crown onto His head, He wore it. When His friends ran and hid, leaving a handful of women to walk the way of the cross, He forgave their fears and came to them when He rose up." Corrie motioned to the phone on the table. "We can't let fear keep us from doing the right thing, sweet girl. Even if it's the hardest thing we've done."

Showing up. Facing Isaiah. Treating his horses.

In the end that's what it came down to. Risking the confrontation for the good of the horses. And if Dr. Hirsch wasn't up on the latest findings, her hesitation could spell even more disaster for Isaiah's family.

Corrie patted her shoulder lightly. "I'm taking Ava and Annie for a stroller ride up to the sheep. They love seeing those woolies, and it does me good to hear them laugh. You go and do what you're trained to do, sweetness. And if you happen to show up a man or two on the way, I am all right with that."

Char picked up the phone and took it off speakerphone. "Liam? I'll be right there, honey."

"Oh, thank you, Char! Thank you!"

If nothing else, at least the boy would know she cared, that his entreaty didn't fall on deaf ears. She grabbed her bag, stowed her meds and headed for the van as Corrie released the brake on the oversize stroller.

The two blonde babies batted their arms and laughed at the thought of going uphill and seeing a yard full of sheep.

Their pure joy was contagious. Happy with so little. Happy with life.

A merry heart doeth good like medicine, but a broken spirit drieth the bones. Wise words from an old Proverb. Could all the anxiety and mean behaviors spring from a broken spirit? And could that spirit ever be mended in a person?

Char didn't know. She'd had twenty-six years on the planet and found that self-absorbed people tended to stay that way, while horses and dogs were more forgiving.

She started the van and headed south, and when she turned into Dancing Meadows a quarter hour later, she put a stern restraint on her emotions.

She was here to do a job. An important job. And if they refused her offer, so be it.

But when she saw Isaiah come out of the broodmare barn, chin down…when he paused and scrubbed a hand to his face and then his neck…

Her heart leaped.

She shoved that reaction aside and drove forward.

The sound of the wheels brought his head up.

He saw her.

His face…oh, his sweet face, lined with worry and dark with concern.

If her help could lessen his burden, she'd give

it, because Corrie was right. The strong don't run and hide or hold a grudge. They stand and fight and help as needed.

She rolled to a stop, shut the engine off and jumped out of the van. Like it or not, she was here to do a job at the request of one of the owners. He might be small, but Liam held a 25 percent stock in this enterprise. She aimed to see that he didn't lose it.

"You came." Isaiah moved her way. "Char, we've got to talk."

"We don't." She spoke in a soft but firm voice as she donned a disposable biohazard suit. "One of your co-owners called me that you've had a viral outbreak here. Is that correct?"

He frowned. "A co-owner?"

"You came!"

A shout from the old barn up the driveway loosened his expression. "Liam called you."

She pulled on boot covers once the suit was in place, taking extra precautions. Then she opened the side of the van and withdrew her med box and a biohazard bag. "Foal loss?"

"Two so far."

"Stupid disease, going for the most vulnerable." She scowled, then asked, "Other symptoms?"

He reached to take the case from her.

She didn't let him, and that made him feel

like even more of a crud. "Fever, nasal discharge. No neurological problems as yet, but we're expecting them."

"Not if I can help it." She walked to the barn quickly, spread a disposable cloth on a stack of hay, then set the med case down. She opened it as John came their way. "Subcutaneous heparin helps block the virus from attacking the nervous system. It's experimental and there are no guarantees, but at this point you have little to lose. We might be able to save the mares. Do I have your permission to treat the symptomatic group twice a day?"

Did she just hand him a lifeline? Because it sure sounded like it.

"Char—"

"Yes or no?" She held his gaze with a flat look, a look he deserved after the scene he created a few days before. She kept it clinical and impersonal because he'd been an absolute moron and had spent too long believing what Braden wanted him to believe. The flowers he'd ordered a few hours ago weren't nearly enough of an apology…but he hoped they would be a beginning.

"Absolutely. I didn't know there was an option."

She turned her attention to the meds. One by one she injected the mares. When she was done and her used vials were stowed in the bag, she looked at her watch. "We want to do this again in eight hours. Then we'll start a morning-evening regimen for the next few days. And then we'll see. I'll be back at nine o'clock."

"You think this can help, Char?" John asked. "It would be a mighty fine thing to save these mares."

"We've had no neurological involvement at Carrington's so far," she told him. "And that outbreak is days ahead of yours. If we've treated it in time, the heparin fights off the replication of virus. But we've just got to wait and see. I'll be back tonight."

She didn't hang around. She removed the biohazard suit and boot covers out in the yard, and then used the sink in her van to scrub up.

Quick. Effective. Up on current medical finds. And he'd insulted her by assuming her guilt in something that wasn't her fault.

She waved to Liam and gave him a thumbs-up, then got into the van.

The boy waved back.

Liam, eight years old and unsure of himself, had the courage to go above Isaiah's head and call Char himself. And if Char's treatment staved off the deadly side of the virus, they'd still have their brood mares.

Yes, they'd have to breed again, but that was

a whole lot better than years spent raising fillies to mares.

John came over and clapped him on the back. And none too lightly, either. "Some advice from an old man," he told Isaiah. "Figure out a way to get that girl to marry you, son, because this whole family could use a daily dose of whatever it is she carries. And that's all I'm saying about that."

"Not as easy as you make it out to be," he told his father. "Not after what I did."

John made a skeptical face. "Courting a woman isn't as difficult as you're making out." He stated the words plainly. "You start with an apology for being stupid, do some well-deserved groveling and end with a proposal. And it never hurts if there's a good dose of chocolate and flowers in between."

"I sent flowers this morning," Isaiah answered.

"It's a start. But a smart man wastes no time, because a woman like that is the kind of woman a man wants by his side. And I'm not even considering the advantage of free veterinary care." John laughed for the first time in days, then went to do his own scrubbing up at the far sink.

It couldn't be that simple.

But that didn't stop him from calling the Rocky Mountain Candy Company and ordering a two-pound box for Pine Ridge.

Char had wasted no time coming to his aid. Now he needed to be just as decisive about winning her heart.

Chapter Fifteen

Two dog calls, one kitten call and a stop at Carrington's to assess progress.

One horse was doing badly. Her deteriorating condition left Char no course of action, but seven horses showed signs of improvement, and that was a huge step forward.

"And no sign in the other barns?"

"None," Ty reported. "Char, I can't tell you how grateful we are. Me, my brother, my dad." He scrubbed a hand to the back of his neck and yawned. "They're knee-deep in running the family business but they love this ranch and these animals. They'll be relieved to know what's happening. How you turned the tide in our favor."

"It's my job, cowboy."

He laughed. "You do it well. Thank you."

A good outcome. Not perfect, but way better than it could have been.

Would she have the same results at Isaiah's place?

Time would tell.

She went back to Pine Ridge. Jace washed the van down for her. She grabbed a shower, and when she came downstairs to fill a to-go cup with sweet tea, a brightly hued summer bouquet brightened the kitchen island. "Stunning arrangement," she noted as she poured the tea. Lizzie was placing a supply order from her laptop, and Corrie was snuggling Ava in a comfy old rocking chair. "Did you do this?" she asked Corrie. She motioned toward the flowers with her free hand.

"No. They arrived a little while ago," Corrie replied. "There's a card, I believe."

There was, tucked between two blossoms. Char leaned closer. Read her name. And then she wasn't sure she even wanted to open the card. But she did.

"Forgive me. Please. It will never happen again, little lady."

No signature, but then it didn't need one. Only one person called her little lady.

The florist hadn't gone all millennial by using unscented flowers. The heady mix of fragrances filled the air surrounding the bouquet.

Not too much. Just enough. Kind of like how life should be.

"A nice gesture, but lacking in chocolate." Lizzie looked up without raising her chin. "I'd be okay if you make him suffer a little more. Nobody picks on my baby sister."

"But they are real pretty," noted Corrie. She flashed a smile Char's way as Ava's eyes grew heavy. Pale lashes fluttered against ivory cheeks, but then the baby's eyes popped open. Startled, she looked up, recognized Corrie and reached up to pat the kind nanny's round cheek. And then she cuddled back in and fell sound asleep.

"I'm a big fan of forgiveness," Corrie went on. "But a little penance can be good for the soul."

"It takes more than flowers to regain lost trust," Char told them flatly.

"Honey, that's where the candy comes in," noted Lizzie. "And it's always wise to send enough to share." She closed the laptop and sent Char a smile. "But that's just me."

"The good Lord wouldn't have put chocolate on the planet if He didn't want us to eat it," said Corrie. "He wants his people happy. But then we knew that."

Did they?

Lizzie and Corrie always seemed secure in their faith, even in the rough times. Was it simplistic?

No. Because there was nothing one-dimensional about either woman.

But there was something inspirational in the way they handled things. Melonie, too, and she'd been walking a tightrope for years, striving to please too many people.

Mel wasn't like that now and she seemed happy. So happy.

Char got into the van and drove to Dancing Meadows a little after eight o'clock. Deepening shadows split the fading light. As she pulled up to the barn, the dusk-to-dawn lights flickered on.

She donned her protective suit and secured the head covering.

She'd have preferred to stride into the barn looking like Veterinarian Barbie, but tonight she looked more like Hazmat Hazel.

Oh, well.

Isaiah was coming her way from the barn. She put her heart on total lockdown, but hearts are fickle things and hers refused to obey.

He looked tired. So tired. But strong, too, as if facing potential disaster in his herd was just another hurdle in life. Maybe after losing people you love, it was.

His gaze softened, and those eyes—those beautiful brown eyes—brightened at the sight of her. "You're early."

"I wanted to have time to suit up and see you."

He squinted slightly in an almost smile. "Wish granted."

"Not exactly a wish," she told him smoothly. "More along lines of necessity. You're a horse owner. I'm a veterinarian. Let's stick to basics here."

He shoved his hands into his pockets and rocked back on his heels as if she was right, and suddenly she didn't want to be right. Stupid fickle heart.

"Got it. How are Ty's horses doing? I left him a voice mail. I'm sure he's worried."

Concerned for his friend, more than himself. Why did that touch her? Because it hadn't existed in the men she'd known.

"Better than expected," she replied. "One horse didn't make it, but the rest are showing signs of recovery."

"Those are way better odds than other ranchers have faced with a herpes breakout."

They were. "Nothing at Scoville's as yet, so maybe they dodged a bullet. And the state is monitoring our progress. The same state—" she turned to face him more fully "—that granted me reciprocal permission to practice here because my name was cleared of any wrongdoing in Central New York. In case you haven't taken the time to discover that yet."

He winced.

Good.

She started to walk past him.

He reached out to take her arm, but she stopped him with ·a look. The look didn't stop him from talking, however. "Char, I was wrong."

He sure was. And he'd assumed the information Braden fed him was correct. Even if it looked legit, he should have come to her. Asked about it.

Or disbelieved the whole thing because you'd never do anything like that.

She liked the mental advice best.

She kept walking. She had a job to do and she'd come to do it. She didn't have to impress him. Or anyone, for that matter. Not anymore. Those days were long gone.

He'd set up a sturdy table for her supplies. He draped the table with gloved hands and stood quietly while she got things ready. And when she finished, she pointed to her watch. "I'm taking first shift tonight." When he started to argue, she tapped it as John came their way. "You two look dreadful. You haven't slept right in days and it shows. Go. Sleep. I've got this. It's not the first time I've monitored a barn and it sure won't be my last."

"I'm not about to refuse that offer," said John,

relieved. "I could use a good four or five hours. You could, too," he told Isaiah. "People talk stupid when they're tired. Maybe a little rest will smarten us men up."

She took a seat on the stacked straw they used for bedding.

John started out of the barn.

Isaiah didn't.

He turned her way. And when he took a spot on the straw, almost close enough to touch her, but didn't...

He tipped his broad-brimmed hat down over his eyes and leaned back. "I'll rest right here, little lady. If you don't mind."

She did mind.

She minded a lot, but they were his horses in his barn. She pulled out a book of crossword puzzles. "Suit yourself."

"Will do."

He fell asleep almost instantly. He snored, just a little, and she wasn't sure why she found that endearing, but she did. And when she got tired of crosswords, she did a quick check of the horses.

All was calm. All was bright...

And then it wasn't.

A whinny sounded outside.

She moved to the paddock area.

The noise came again, an equine call for help.

The old barn, out front. Ginger. And both men sound asleep and her in the infected barn.

The mare cried again.

Char reached for her phone to call J.J. The girl would be in a better position to help the mare than the two exhausted men. She started placing the call, then paused.

A figure was hurrying toward the barn. Short. Somewhat stout. She moved on quick feet, and when she passed beneath the dusk-to-dawn yard light, Stella Woods' features flashed briefly. And then she was in the far barn.

Char stared at the barn, torn. What was going on? What was Isaiah's mother doing there, at this moment?

Stella hated that horse. She'd made that plain. Was she in there to do harm while everyone slept? Would she do such a thing?

Char didn't know, but Isaiah would. She started back toward the broodmare barn, then paused when she heard a voice. Not an angry voice. A soft, melodic voice, almost crooning, and on the night breeze came the words Char knew so well. Only this time it was another mother singing them, and it wasn't to a lonely little girl.

The old words were being sung to a pregnant old horse. "Hushabye… Don't you cry… Go to sleep, little lady. When you wake, you shall have all the pretty little horses…"

Stella came into view again. She'd haltered Ginger and was walking her around the small grazing area. And as she and the aged mare plodded along, she softly and sweetly continued the song.

She hadn't come to hurt the horse.

She'd come to help. And at that moment, across the expanse of grass and gravel, she raised her eyes. Saw Char watching. And when she did, she raised one hand in salute, reassuring Char that all was well.

And as Char slipped her phone back into her pocket, she was pretty sure she was right.

Isaiah's arm had fallen asleep over an hour ago, about the time Char nodded off beside him.

He didn't move it. Didn't try to shift to ease the strain. Letting her rest was more important.

A horse moved.

The shadows shifted and Char jerked up. She blinked, saw the dawn breaking and him watching her, and sat up more fully. "I dozed off."

"Wasn't much to see at that point. Everything's quiet."

She realized that he'd had his arm around her, supporting her. She started to pull away as her phone buzzed a message. She picked it up.

A picture came through. Ginger and a long-legged chestnut foal with white legs, a perfect image in an imperfect world. She held up her phone for him to see. "Look."

He gazed at the picture, surprised. "Who sent it? J.J.?"

"Your mother."

He stared at her, then the picture, then her again. "My mother helped Ginger?"

"While you were sleeping."

He couldn't believe it. In the old days that wouldn't have surprised him. His mother used to be a big part of the ranch. The cattle, the horses, the family. Stella Woods had been woven into the fabric of the ranch. But when they lost Alfie, she'd stepped away and hadn't found her way back in over twenty years.

Today she had.

"Mother and daughter doing well. No complications. Beautiful baby." Char read him the text as she shrugged away from his arm. Away from him.

He didn't want her away from him.

He'd known that all along.

Was it crazy to believe in love at first sight? Or to risk a life on destiny?

Then he'd like to be crazy, because he'd never felt like this before. As if she—this amazing woman—was meant for him.

She stood and brushed bits of straw from her disposable suit. He stood, too. The sun was just breaking light over the eastern mountains—a new day welcoming them.

Char checked the horses. "No signs of neuro involvement," she told him as she went down the line. "On anyone. So far, so good."

No signs.

He moved toward her and hugged her. Just that. And not because of his feelings for her, although those were substantial.

She'd jumped in when not invited. Taken charge. Brought him help he didn't even know existed.

"Hey." She moved to step back. Her voice held a warning.

"This isn't a romantic hug," he assured her, and he absolutely, positively did not let go. "It's a hug of gratitude."

She pulled back, anyway. "Send a card," she advised. "You know my address."

"Isaiah!" J.J. called his name from the barn down front. "You won't believe what happened!"

He moved around the front of the barn and waved acknowledgment.

"Ginger's got the prettiest foal with white feet and I want to name her Ginger Stockings. What do you think?"

His mother came out of the barn right then. She took her place beside J.J. And when she gazed at him across the expanse of meadow separating them, it wasn't the angry woman he was used to who was looking back.

It was the old Stella. His mother. Her true self.

She sent him a text. When you are all scrubbed up, come to our house. Making breakfast. Bring doctor.

He sent her back a thumbs-up emoji. J.J. stayed at the barn with Ginger and the foal. His mother walked up the path toward her house.

Liam poked a head around the far barn door.

His mother had let Liam come into the barn while she tended the horse.

She'd turned a corner after all these years.

He went back to the barn. "My mother is making us breakfast."

"What?" She looked up from her electronic notebook, brows raised.

She looked ridiculous in that funny suit. And amazingly beautiful because she cared enough to go the extra mile. To do her job to the best of her ability.

Then she nodded as if the news of his mother and the horse and the foal made her happy. "I'll head home after this early injection so you guys can have some family time."

"She gave strict instructions to bring you." He

moved closer as she set up for the morning injections. "And after she stepped in to help with Ginger's foaling, I don't want to step on toes."

She frowned. "I don't think she really wants me there, Isaiah."

He stepped in front of her before she got to the next horse. "She does. We all do. Please?" He raised his eyebrow a little. Just enough so she could read the sincerity in his eyes, in his question. "You went the distance, Char." He held her gaze. "You put my stupid behavior aside and did what needed to be done, and I don't know a lot of folks who would do that. But you did. And breakfast is just one way of showing you how much that means to us. And it will make Liam happy."

"Such a good boy." She hesitated, clearly torn.

He didn't want to coerce her. She was here for a year and that bought him time. Time to make amends. Mend bridges. Apologize repeatedly, if necessary.

But when she raised her eyes to his…and said yes to breakfast…he felt like he might be back on the right path, after all.

Chapter Sixteen

"Someone's smitten," noted Lizzie later that week. She scanned the two-layer box and helped herself to the third chocolate of the morning. "A two-pound box from the Rocky Mountain Chocolate Factory isn't just a thank-you, darling." She shoulder-nudged Char as walked by. "It's more like a promise."

"Almost a proposal," noted Melonie. "Char, you've got a few minutes. Can you feed Annie while I feed Ava? I've got to make a list of things we need to order for their birthday party and I can't seem to get five minutes to do it."

Char had managed not to feed small humans in the few weeks she'd been here, but it appeared her hands-off days had come to an end. She hit Send on her supply order and slipped into a chair. "Okay. I've got this. How hard can it be?" she asked no one in particular.

She picked up the bowl of mush, an interesting concoction of yogurt, baby cereal and mashed banana. "Here you go." She raised the spoon.

Annie slapped the spoon. The baby's quick action spattered Char, the high chair, the table and herself with sticky cereal as the spoon went flying.

"Annie Middleton, no, no, no." Melonie squatted down, met the baby eye to eye and scolded. "That was naughty. No hit." She kept her voice firm and held the baby's gaze like you would a much older child.

Annie stared at Melonie. Her eyes went wide. Her lower lip bulged out and the sweet baby girl looked absolutely heartbroken.

Char's gut twisted. She had to fight the urge to rescue the baby. She turned toward Mel in disbelief while Lizzie got a fresh spoon. "You just yelled at a baby," she hissed as wheels crunched on the driveway outside. "How can you do that and live with yourself, Mel?"

"Easy peasy," replied her sister. "I watched you break horses, remember?"

Char winced.

She could be as strong as needed when it came to breaking young horses into socially acceptable creatures. But babies?

The very thought of disciplining the girls

scared her. "She's so little." She whispered the words so Annie wouldn't hear the sympathy in her voice. "She's a baby."

"Gotta love a novice," noted Lizzie as she made her second cup of coffee. The coffee brewed…she smelled it…and then dumped it. "Did anyone else notice the coffee smells awful this morning?"

"Mine was great," replied Char as she accepted the clean spoon from Lizzie.

Melonie shook her head. "Mine's fine." She sipped her coffee to prove her point, then stood. "Give it a try again and let's see if Miss Annie will behave."

Char dipped the spoon into the cereal.

Annie watched the spoon come her way. She raised her little hand, then caught Melonie's eye…

And she put her hand down.

"Mel. You did it!" Char fed the baby a spoonful, and once Annie got a taste of it, there was no more slapping of the spoon. "It worked. Yelling at a baby worked."

"I spoke firmly. No yelling involved," Mel told her as she fed Ava.

The doorbell rang.

The little dog Lizzie had rescued in the spring leaped out of her bed and charged the door, tail wagging.

"Who's here at eight thirty in the morning?"

"And who rings the doorbell?" wondered Melonie. "I didn't even know this house had a doorbell."

They heard Corrie go to the door. A minute later she appeared in the wide kitchen with Isaiah's mother.

Char had to work double time to hide her surprise. "Mrs. Woods, good morning." She started to get up but Isaiah's mother waved her down and then she did something even more surprising. She sat down next to Char and set a big box of cookies on the table. "For you. For all of you," she said, including the women in her look. "I came over to say I'm sorry, Charlotte."

The baby squealed in protest because Char had stopped feeding her.

Lizzie lifted a clean mug as Char resumed her duties to keep the baby happy. "May I get you coffee, Mrs. Woods?"

"I would like that," Stella told her as Annie squawked again. The noise made Stella smile. And then she sighed softly. "I have wasted a lot of time." She looked at Corrie as if the older woman would understand and Corrie nodded.

"So many years of anger," she went on. "And disrespect. I hid my own mistakes while I chastised others." Sadness gripped her features, but something else lurked behind the sadness. A hint of unexpected tranquility. "My family and my people love this land. All of it." She waved an expansive hand toward the back door. "I got so mad when strangers moved in, buying settlers' land and tribal farms. I felt cheated. My father's family sold their land to Sean Fitzgerald when he first came to town. They needed retirement money and Sean wanted to build a ranch. Startin' over, he said, and he had a marine's swagger when he said it. A swagger that showed a confidence I envied.

"I didn't want them to sell," she continued. "I wanted them to hold on. Wait until things got better. We argued, again and again, but my father was tired. Tired of fighting the land, tired of barely scraping out a living. And so the land was sold. Ours. And others. And my anger grew."

"And that's when we must discern if it's love of land or lust for land?" said Corrie softly. "The wanting of things can be our downfall. We know that well in this family."

"You've got a beautiful ranch," said Char as she continued to feed the baby. "Yours and Isaiah's. They're as pretty as anything I ever saw in Kentucky."

Stella faced her more directly. "That's because John's family clung tight to their land in the hard times. They increased their ranch and their side businesses. They are hardworking people, always building toward the future."

Like Isaiah, Char thought. He had that steady, strong work ethic that moved day by day. An ethic she not only admired, but one she shared.

"I was spoiled," Stella admitted as Lizzie set her coffee down. She smiled her thanks and added cream and sugar. "I was an only child and clung to too much. I felt like my legacy was being given away while John's stayed strong, and I let it eat at me as if we weren't connected by tribe and marriage. And then my nephew was lost in a terrible accident when I startled his horse and my anger grew. Not at myself, of course." Aggravation tinged her voice. "At God. At others. It was always someone else's fault. Only now it's time to mend those old wrongs."

"No better time at all," said Corrie and she gave Stella's arm a light squeeze.

"Liam keeps talking about this place," Stella told them. "How beautiful it is. And I see what is happening at the Hardaway Ranch, how Jace is rebuilding his grandmother's house and the ranch. It will be lovely again, but Lord forgive me, I was happy as I watched it disintegrate. Their failure felt like my reward, and I'm sorry about that because it was a stupid way to live and a horrible example to set for my children and my grandchildren."

"Fortunately children are resilient," said Corrie. She smiled at the three young women, and Char understood the truth behind her words. Corrie's love and faith had built their strengths, and that had prepared them for their father's later deceit. So maybe that chance meeting of Corrie with their mother wasn't a coincidence at all. Maybe God put the two women together then to ensure the girls' futures now.

He hath made everything beautiful in its time... The verse from *Ecclesiastes* stirred her. Was this all about timing? God's timing? Allowing things to happen as they should?

"I robbed them of good memories," said Stella softly. She gazed down at her hands, then brought her head up in a way that made her look more like Isaiah. "But that's over. Now I will help as Isaiah raises Andrew's children in the church. As he teaches J.J. to jump and Liam to work horses with no fear. No trepidation. Just love and respect."

She reached out a hand to Char's arm. "I made property more important than people. I made my reputation more important, as well. I was foolish. And I'm sorry that I made trouble for you. For my son."

"Well, there's no need for blame, is there?"

asked Corrie softly. "Just a need for forgiveness, maybe."

"Forgiveness and atonement." Stella folded her hands. "I've gone to my brother and sister-in-law and explained everything about my nephew's accident. And they didn't hate me, although they could have. Maybe should have."

Her nephew. Alfie. The child lost when the horse shied years ago.

"They said they were sorry." Her eyes flashed. "So sorry, and I said why? And they said…" Her eyes filled. She sat there, trying to stave the tears and failing. "'Because the guilt and sorrow have cost you so much time. Our boy is in heaven, and we'll see him again, but we would have never caused you so much pain, dear Stella.'" More tears slipped down her cheeks.

Lizzie handed her a box of tissues. Stella grabbed two and dabbed her cheeks. Her eyes.

"Bah, bah, bah!" Annie waved her arms to signal she was done.

Stella smiled and swiped her eyes again. "I didn't mean to get so emotional."

"Well, we're Southern girls," noted Char, purposely easing the moment. "Emotional roller coasters are our favorite rides. How is Ginger's foal doing?" She hadn't dared go near the front barn to see for herself until all lingering traces of herpes had been wiped clean.

"A lovely girl. And the mama horse has perked up considerably. Having a young one around keeps us on our toes."

"It does keep us young." Corrie laughed as she washed Annie's sweet face. "Because there's no time to grow old when life keeps blossoming around us."

"Exactly that." Stella finished her coffee and stood as Zeke barged in through the back door.

"Cookies? Can I have one? Me and Harve Jr. are checking fence," the little guy boasted. "It's real important and we might be gone a long while," he added as Lizzie handed him four cookies. He stared at the cookies, eyes wide.

"Two for you. Two for Junior. Cowboys need to keep up their strength. And can you thank Mrs. Woods, please? She brought us these lovely cookies."

Zeke didn't just thank Stella. He threw his arms around her in a hug of huge proportions. "Thank you for bringing us cookies! We'll love these so much!" He raced back out before she could respond. The door banged shut behind him, a five-year-old whirlwind of pure energy.

Stella stared after him, then smiled. "He is all boy. Like our Liam. Beautiful. Bright. Busy."

"All of the above," agreed Lizzie, smiling.

Char lifted Annie from the chair and handed her to Corrie. "Mrs. Woods? Would you like me to show you around Pine Ridge?" she asked as she washed up. It took a minute to locate and wipe down all of the baby's initial spatter spots.

"I would. Yes. But it's Stella. Please."

"Well, then." Char wiped her hands dry, then offered her right hand in greeting, as if they hadn't met before. "Hey, Stella. I'm Char Fitzgerald, a new veterinarian in town. It's a pleasure to meet you."

Stella's smile grew. She took Char's hand, accepting the initiative. "And I'm Stella Woods. The pleasure is all mine."

She shook Char's hand, and when Char led the way out the back door, it wasn't like walking side by side with a former adversary.

It was like walking side by side with a new friend.

Chapter Seventeen

The horses were recovering.

Three foals lost, but their mothers survived.

No traces of virus found in two weeks and no further horses affected.

Isaiah hauled in a breath he'd been holding for nearly a month, then pulled out his phone when it signaled a text. On my way to do final symptom check. ETA fifteen minutes.

Char was on her way.

His hands went sweaty.

He swiped them against his pant legs.

He looked around the adjacent pasture, a pasture that would look quite different without her intervention. After today he would move the horses. One last checkup and the quarantine would be lifted. And while they'd suffered some loss, it was minimal compared to what could have happened.

He owed Char. Big-time. More than he could ever repay because it wasn't just about the financial end of things. She'd made a difference here. A difference to his family, his ranch and to the town. And with Labor Day and the return to school approaching, he wanted to face the approaching autumn with her.

She pulled into the yard three minutes earlier than she'd expected, which meant she was driving too fast, hopefully because she was excited to see him.

She climbed out of the van and didn't don the protective suit. Another good sign.

She looked amazing.

His heart sped up. His hands got sweaty all over again. And when she turned and spotted him, she paused.

So did his heart.

She moved forward as he held up a printout of a brief announcement posted on the tribal Facebook page. "Braden has announced his retirement."

She frowned. "Because of me?"

"Because the spread of infection was traced back to his brother. He'd accompanied Braden on farm visits earlier this summer, hoping to scare up votes for the November elections. Only, he had the virus working on his place and didn't know it at the time. And once he realized, he tried to cover it up because he feared the ranch owners would punish him at the polls."

"And inadvertently spread it to other barns. I'm sure Braden had no idea," she added. "No veterinarian would take that chance. He probably feels dreadful."

Kind. Caring. Forgiving. And empathetic to the man who had tried to blackball her.

His heart beat a little harder and a whole lot faster as she drew near.

She smelled of vanilla and fresh air. Of sunshine and warmth. And she looked great in her jeans and short-sleeved T-shirt. She drew up to the rail, set her bag down and breathed deeply as she leaned against the wooden fencing. "There's a freshness to the air today."

"There is." He moved alongside her and rested his arms on the top rail. Just like she did. "Not quite fall but you can tell it's coming. In the tops of the trees." He pointed to where the uppermost leaves were already hinting color. "And the grass, a little greener now that we've gotten some rain. And the dew."

"I sopped my sneakers this morning, unknowing," she told him. And then she looked at him. Right at him. And he realized he wanted that. Her. Looking at him. Sharing with him. By his side. "Should have worn boots, first thing. Now I know."

"Are we really talking about sneakers?" He turned and rested his back against the top rail so he could see her. Hold her gaze. "When there's so much more to say?"

So much more to say...

She started to turn, to reach for her bag...

He paused her with one arm. One big, solid cowboy arm. "I'm sorry, Char."

She could have backed up. Ducked away.

She didn't.

He touched her hair. Then her cheek. Gentle. So gentle. Yet strong, too, in so many ways. "I was stupid."

No argument there. She didn't look up at him. She kept her gaze averted purposely.

"And I can't even guarantee I won't be stupid again."

She turned now, surprised, because what kind of apology was that?

The hand touching her hair grazed her cheek softly. He smiled. "In fact I can almost guarantee it, bein' a man and all. But if you could forgive me—"

"For thinking I was a horse-swindling jerk who cheated people for my own selfish ends."

"It does sound awful, doesn't it?" He leaned his forehead to hers.

Her heart sped up. He smelled soap-and-water

good, which meant he'd deliberately cleaned up after doing morning chores, because four hours in horse barns didn't generally smell like fresh linens, hung to dry.

But he did smell like that. Just like that and she wanted to lean in closer. Breathe him in. And then...

She was kissing him.

She wasn't sure who turned their face first, and it didn't matter. All that mattered right now was here. Right here, in this graveled barnyard surrounding these now-healthy horses.

Him.

This.

Them. And two kids who were searching for their place in the world.

"Char." He whispered her name as he peppered her face with kisses, and when he rubbed his cheek along hers and then kissed her again, Char was pretty sure that she and the pricey van would never be leaving Shepherd's Crossing. "I love you, Char."

Did he really? Could he, after so short a time? And yet didn't she feel exactly the same?

"I think this is where you say 'I love you, too, Isaiah,'" he whispered into her ear. "Because, woman... I know you do. And there's only one way to handle this whole thing, little lady."

She smiled against his mouth. His lips. "And what's that, cowboy?"

"Well, to marry the girl, of course."

Her smile widened.

"Bring her on home, have a baby or two. Raise up the youngsters. And when you throw free veterinary care in on top, that's a sound deal all the way around."

She smacked his arm, but laughed when she did it.

And then kissed him again. And when she stopped kissing him, she leaned back, against his arm. "Is this your proposal, Isaiah?"

"Unless you want a fancy dinner…"

"They tend to give me indigestion," she told him.

His smile grew. "More flowers?"

"It seems the good Lord has provided a plethora of those." She nodded toward the hills rising to the east, with the pinks and yellows and whites of late-summer wildflowers painting their own picture.

"Music?"

"Not when I'd rather hear your voice. Your words," she whispered up to him. "Best music there is."

"We should at least have a ring," he supposed, and then he reached into his pocket and withdrew a little black velvet box. "Which it seems I have. Right here."

Her heart went into steeplechase rhythm. Fast. Jumping. Elated. "Isaiah."

"Will you marry me, Char? Be my helpmate? My love? My life?"

Laughter came their way just then. J.J. and Liam, working together with Ginger and her foal.

The perfect package, she realized. Imperfect, of course, but just right for her. Which meant God's timing had been guiding her here, to this moment, all along. "I will be thrilled to marry you, Isaiah." She wrapped her hands around his neck and leaned up for one more kiss. "And be here with you every day." Another kiss. "And every night."

That got her a grin and a kiss.

"But I will charge you for veterinary care, my love, because after all—" she reached up and tweaked the brim of his broad cowboy hat "—business is business."

He laughed.

So did she.

And when he slipped the solitary diamond onto her finger—a perfect fit—she didn't just feel like she'd come home at last.

She knew it. And that was the best feeling of all.

Epilogue

"Are we taking the salad and both cakes?" Isaiah asked as Char hurried down the stairs the next July, and he didn't try to disguise the longing in his voice. "Because it would be okay to leave a cake here, wouldn't it?"

"It's a patriotic cake auction, and both have to go," she told him, then paused when he reached out, grabbed her around the waist and drew her in.

He kissed her. Maybe to talk her into leaving a cake behind, or maybe just to kiss her. Either way she melted into the kiss like she'd been doing since their fall wedding.

And then he laid one hand over her still-flat abdomen and raised those thick eyebrows. "I think the baby will want cake later, darling. So we should leave one at home."

She burst out laughing, then hugged him.

Hugged him tightly. When she drew back, she raised one hand and the pointer finger. "This is clear evidence that husbands do not listen well. The whole idea of a cake auction is that we donate cakes…"

"I get that part." He looked glum on purpose as he gave the whipped-cream-and-berry patriotic cake a sad glance.

"And then we buy other cakes to raise money to refurbish the Veteran's Outreach Center. So the money goes for a good cause and we still end up with cake. And—" she hooked a thumb toward the backup refrigerator in the garage "—I may have made two of the whipped cream cakes you love so well, so the one in the extra fridge stays here."

Relief flooded his features. "Your organizational skills are only one reason I love you."

"And the others?" She batted her eyelashes like the total Southern girl she was. "Tell me true, cowboy."

"Too many to list," he answered, grinning. "But I promise to show you later." He winked as he took the cakes to the running car. He'd moved it to the shade and turned on the air-conditioning. The meteorologists had predicted a fairly hot Independence Day, and Char didn't want the food to be spoiled by the heat.

"I'm ready." J.J. came into the kitchen, looking like a Western ad for patriotism. She wore a stars-and-stripes top over white shorts and red, white and blue sandals she'd gotten online. "Anything you need, Char?"

"Your brother?"

J.J. laughed. "Outside with Rising, of course." She went to the door and called them in.

Rising loped along as if he'd never been hurt, and a taller Liam followed.

"Are we really going to find out if the baby's a boy or a girl at the picnic today?" he asked, first thing.

Isaiah came back inside. He ruffled Liam's hair and let Char take lead. "Well, that's when everyone else will find out, but we wanted you guys to know first."

"For real?" Liam's eyes went wide and he jumped up, fist-pumping the air. "I love this!"

J.J. squealed. "I've been dying to know since you found out," she told them. "So, what is it?"

"A boy," Isaiah told them. "A little boy that we'll name Andrew, if that's all right with you guys."

"All right?" J.J.'s eyes went damp. "I think it's awesome." She hugged them both in turn. "I love it. Dad would be so happy for you."

"He would," Isaiah agreed. He turned toward Liam. "What do you think, Liam?"

"I think it will be the best Thanksgiving present ever." He reached out and hugged Char. And he didn't let go. "Can I help do things with him? When he gets bigger? Like show him things and teach him things like Dad and Uncle Isaiah did with me?"

Char exchanged a satisfied look with Isaiah, over the boy's head. "Exactly what we're hoping," Char assured him. "That way he'll be learning from the best."

Liam hugged her tighter, then sighed. "I'm so glad you're here."

She hugged him back. "Me, too. Ready to go?"

"Yes! And I'll stay secret until you tell everybody, okay?"

She laughed and didn't correct his speech because *stay secret* worked for this special day. "Perfect."

They drove into Shepherd's Crossing for the first annual Independence Day celebration, sponsored by Pine Ridge Ranch and the Veteran's Association.

Patriotic banners hung from the arches of new businesses.

Flags hung from the newly painted streetlights along the abbreviated Main Street, and eight new planters sat proudly on the sidewalk, filled with eye-catching blossoms.

Windows gleamed from every building, and

the small white church showed off its heightened activity with two wooden benches tucked alongside hosta-filled shade gardens, each inviting repose.

The church bell pealed from the small tower. Ty and Jess Carrington came out below. Dovie, Jess's daughter, dashed ahead of them. She spun to show off a red, white and blue sundress, the image of a happy child.

An aging army veteran waved them into the parking lot at the old general store.

Melonie and Jace had purchased the old building earlier that year. They planned to refurbish the building and bring it back to its original purpose once Melonie's morning sickness subsided.

Change surrounded them, thought Char, as J.J. and Liam carried cakes to the refrigerated cooler Heath had rigged outside the door of the old grocery store.

People had come from all over, toting dishes of this and that.

Char took the salad to the picnic buffet table, where Lizzie, Corrie, Stella, Sally Ann and Melonie were busily organizing the foods of the day. Gilda Hardaway was off to one side, directing things, while she pushed the twins in a double stroller.

"This," she told them with an almost stern

wave of her hand. "This is what little towns were meant for. Folks gathering together, working together, getting things done. Now, doesn't this look just fine?" she asked them all. "So fine."

"It looks marvelous," Melonie replied. "What a huge difference from last year. And so many more good things to come."

Char knew what she meant. Revitalizing the town was a big deal to Melonie, and to Jace, and to all the people who'd watched the little town go downhill for so long.

But for her...

She smiled as Isaiah and Liam carried their folding table to the shaded corner of the small park setting.

It wasn't about the town, although that was a bonus.

It was about people. About family. About faith and the normal she'd longed for all those years ago.

Isaiah stopped on his way back to get a half dozen folding chairs from his parents' truck. He paused...

Smiled...

And then kissed her, right there, in the middle of everyone. And when he was done kissing her, he touched the brim of that hat and smiled. "Welcome home, Char."

He knew. He understood. And he cared that her dream of normal had finally come true. She smiled and raised her hand to bump knuckles with his. "It's mighty good to be here, cowboy."

The veterans lined up to lead a little parade to the new flagpole the Carringtons had donated. Today they would hoist a flag that had flown over the White House. The flag would take its place of prominence in Shepherd's Crossing. And when they began marching up the road, people followed. All kinds of people, old and new, ready to call this town their own.

And mixed in with them were the three Fitzgerald sisters and their new families. Were they brought to town by their uncle's generosity and wisdom?

Maybe.

But most of all by God's perfect timing.

And at the day's end, when the whole gathering reacted to beautiful fireworks donated by none other than Gilda Hardaway, Char sank back into Isaiah's strong arms. They'd spread blankets on the ground as Ty and his brother engineered the fireworks display across the field.

"Happy?" He whispered the question into her ear as Liam jumped up and down and J.J. cheered while Stella and John sat in folding chairs to their right.

She tipped her head back. Met his gaze. "The happiest."

He smiled back. Kissed her gently. And then laid his hands over their unborn child, a swimmer in a secret sea. "Me, too. And when this little guy gets born, I'm going to tell him what a difference his mother made. How she made everything better. Brighter. Bolder."

"Before or after you change his diaper?"

He laughed and nuzzled her cheek gently. "Both, my love. Both."

* * * * *

If you loved this story,
don't miss the other books
in the Shepherd's Crossing series
from author Ruth Logan Herne.

Her Cowboy Reunion
"Falling for the Christmas Cowboy"
from A Cowboy Christmas

A Cowboy in Shepherd's Crossing

Available now from Love Inspired!

Find more great reads at
www.LoveInspired.com

Dear Reader,

Thank you so much for reading this beautiful romance! I love Char and Isaiah's story, and not for the obvious happy ending, but for the mix of cultures and thoughts that become our normal because we live them…and sometimes we don't see that "normal" can be a relative thing.

Isaiah is a peacemaker, but he's strong, too. He wants a happy family and he's sacrificed to encourage that.

Char has longed for a happy family all of her life. In her eyes that's the normal she craves. Not expecting to find that in Idaho, she doesn't come west with illusions. Where better than the American West to polish a horse vet's expertise, to build her résumé?

But people can be petty or angry anywhere, and when faced with animosity, Char has a lot on her plate. She doesn't measure success in dollars. She grew up seeing the futility in that. But she's practical enough to know a gal's got to pay her bills and that requires clientele with patients.

I hope you love this book. I've thoroughly enjoyed working in this town and with these families, and I hope you've treasured their stories!

You know I love hearing from readers,

so email me at loganherne@gmail.com or friend me on Facebook and/or follow me on Twitter, @RuthLoganHerne. And my bosses love it if you follow me on Bookbub! Just go here and click follow: https://www.bookbub.com/authors/ruth-logan-herne.

And may God bless you and yours each and every day!

Ruthy

Get 4 FREE REWARDS!

We'll send you 2 FREE Books plus 2 FREE Mystery Gifts.

Love Inspired® Suspense books feature Christian characters facing challenges to their faith... and lives.

FREE Value Over **$20**

BETTY NEELS COLLECTION!

Buy 3 and get 1 FREE!

Experience one of the most celebrated and beloved authors in romance! Betty Neels will delight you with her signature brand of storytelling: happy romances, memorable couples and timeless tales of lasting love. These classics have been combined in 2-in-1 books for your reading pleasure!

YES! Please send me the **Betty Neels Collection**. This collection begins with 4 books, 1 of which is FREE! Plus a FREE gift – an elegant simulated Pearl Necklace & Earring Set (approx. retail value of $13.99). I may either return the shipment and owe nothing or keep for the low members-only discount price of $17.97 U.S./$20.25 CDN plus $1.99 U.S./$2.99 CDN for shipping and handling per shipment.* If I decide to continue, I'll receive two more shipments, each about a month apart, each containing four more two-in-one books, one of which will be free, until I own the entire 12-book collection. Each shipment is mine to keep for the same members-only discount price plus shipping and handling. I understand that no purchase is required. I may keep the free book no matter what I decide.

☐ 275 HCN 4623   ☐ 475 HCN 4623

Name (please print)

Address   Apt. #

City   State/Province   Zip/Postal Code

Mail to the **Reader Service**:
IN U.S.A.: P.O. Box 1341, Buffalo, NY, 14240-8531
IN CANADA: P.O. Box 603, Fort Erie, Ontario L2A 5X3

*Terms and prices subject to change without notice. Prices do not include sales taxes, which will be charged (if applicable) based on your state or country of residence. Canadian residents will be charged applicable taxes. Offer not valid in Quebec. All orders subject to approval. Credit or debit balances in a customer's account(s) may be offset by any other outstanding balance owed by or to the customer. Please allow 3 to 4 weeks for delivery. Offer available while quantities last. © 2019 Harlequin Enterprises Limited.

Your Privacy—The Reader Service is committed to protecting your privacy. Our Privacy Policy is available online at www.ReaderService.com or upon request from the Reader Service. We make a portion of our mailing list available to reputable third parties that offer products we believe may interest you. If you prefer that we not exchange your name with third parties, or if you wish to clarify or modify your communication preferences, please visit us at www.ReaderService.com/consumerchoice or write to us at Reader Service Preference Service, P.O. Box 9062, Buffalo, NY 14269-9062. Include your name and address.

MBN19

COMING NEXT MONTH FROM
Love Inspired®

Available July 16, 2019

THE AMISH BACHELOR'S CHOICE
by Jocelyn McClay
When her late father's business is sold, Ruth Fisher plans on leaving her Amish community to continue her education. But as she helps transition the business into Malachi Schrock's hands, will her growing connection with the handsome new owner convince her to stay?

THE NANNY'S SECRET BABY
Redemption Ranch • by Lee Tobin McClain
In need of a nanny for his adopted little boy, Jack DeMoise temporarily hires his deceased wife's sister. But Jack doesn't know Arianna Shrader isn't just his son's aunt—she's his biological mother. Can she find a way to reveal her secret...and become a permanent part of this little family?

ROCKY MOUNTAIN MEMORIES
Rocky Mountain Haven • by Lois Richer
After an earthquake kills her husband and leaves her with amnesia, Gemma Andrews returns to her foster family's retreat to recuperate. But with her life shaken, she didn't plan on bonding with the retreat's handyman, Jake Elliott...or with her late husband's secret orphaned stepdaughter.

A RANCHER TO REMEMBER
Montana Twins • by Patricia Johns
If Olivia Martin can convince her old friend Sawyer West to reconcile with his former in-laws and allow them into his twins' lives, they will pay for her mother's hospital bills. There's just one problem: an accident wiped everything—including Olivia—from Sawyer's memory. Can she help him remember?

THE COWBOY'S TWIN SURPRISE
Triple Creek Cowboys • by Stephanie Dees
After a whirlwind Vegas romance, barrel racer Lacey Jenkins ends up secretly married and pregnant—with twins. Now can her rodeo cowboy husband, Devin Cole, ever win her heart for real?

A SOLDIER'S PRAYER
Maple Springs • by Jenna Mindel
When she's diagnosed with cancer, Monica Zelinsky heads to her uncle's cabin for a weekend alone to process—and discovers her brother's friend Cash Miller already there with his two young nephews. Stranded together by a storm, will Monica and Cash finally allow their childhood crushes to grow into something more? _____

LOOK FOR THESE AND OTHER LOVE INSPIRED BOOKS WHEREVER BOOKS ARE SOLD, INCLUDING MOST BOOKSTORES, SUPERMARKETS, DISCOUNT STORES AND DRUGSTORES.

LILPCNMBPA0719